# THE BEAST OF WHIXALL MOSS

"A very unusual imaginative book." *Books for Keeps*
"A strange but evocative blend of myth and adventure." *BBC Family Life*

Whixall Moss is in Shropshire, where Pauline Fisk has lived for twenty-five years, and which often features in her books. The idea for the beast itself came on a train journey. "I noticed a man walking through a field with several greyhounds on leads," she says. "For a startling moment they looked like one creature with many heads." The image remained with her and eventually she wrote the story of Jack and the extraordinary beast that enthralls him. "The book is about the fabulous," she says, "and it's about desire."

Pauline Fisk has written several other novels, including *Midnight Blue*, *Telling the Sea* and *Tyger Pool*. *Midnight Blue* won the Smarties Book Prize and was shortlisted for the Whitbread Children's Novel Award. She and her family live in an eighteenth-century town gaol, complete with the remains of cells, within the medieval walls of Shrewsbury – about which she hopes to write more in the future.

Books by the same author

*Midnight Blue*
*Telling the Sea*
*Tyger Pool*

# THE BEAST OF WHIXALL MOSS

### PAULINE FISK

## WALKER BOOKS
**AND SUBSIDIARIES**

LONDON • BOSTON • SYDNEY

*For Bridget, Dory and Chris*

First published 1997 by Walker Books Ltd
87 Vauxhall Walk, London SE11 5HJ

This edition published 1998

2 4 6 8 10 9 7 5 3 1

Text © 1997 Pauline Fisk
Cover illustration © 1997 Christian Birmingham

This book has been typeset in Sabon.

Printed in England

British Library Cataloguing in Publication Data
A catalogue record for this book is
available from the British Library.

ISBN 0-7445-6013-6

# CONTENTS

1   The Year of the Beast                        7

2   Midsummer Time                              16

3   A Garden in a Single Flower                 22

4   Bully Boy                                    29

5   Go quickly – this is your chance            35

6   Questions                                    45

7   Uncle Pip                                    53

8   Betrayal                                     66

9   Knotweed                                     75

10  As if it Never Was                          84

11  A Perfect Day                                88

12  The Transaction                             97

13  The Price                                   108

14  Abalone                                     116

# THE YEAR OF
# THE BEAST

The first was the year of darkness because Jack couldn't remember anything, not anything at all, and the second was the year of light because that was all he could remember. The third was the year of measles, lying in his cot up in the frosty bedroom under the eaves for what felt like ever, and the fourth was the year of his baby brother, Edward.

The fifth was a year of Edward, too, and so was every year after it, but they were years of other things too: the fifth of school, the sixth of seeing what his home was like compared to everybody else's – how far from everywhere it was and, despite Mum's efforts to keep it nice, how small and cramped – the seventh a summer-long year of sports which his dad wanted him to play, what with his memories of his own happy days. But Jack was no good at them, just as he was no good at so many things, always stumbling about, always breaking things, his feet too big, his ears sticking out.

It was in the eighth year that Jack realized that his mother was angry with him. He didn't care to think about why, but in the ninth year his brother started school and then, watching Edward enjoying his lessons, learning the stupid, poxy violin, doing all the things that he, Jack, couldn't do, it seemed to him that his mother was less angry.

In the tenth year, it came to him that what Mum wanted was her own perfect world, no less. She strove for it vigorously. It was her crock of gold at the end of the rainbow, it was her "pearl of great price". But by the eleventh year Jack had realized that the price – pearl or no pearl – was too high. The world wasn't perfect – and it was probably his fault.

Then, in the twelfth year – just when he thought that there was nothing else in life to find out about, when the world seemed fixed, for better or for worse – in the twelfth year two things happened. The first was his baby sister, Emily. And the second was his stumbling, in that clumsy way of his, across the beast. The fabulous and unexpected, the never-to-be-forgotten beast.

Beyond Mum's grim struggle for perfection, and Dad's striving to secure it for her and make everything all right, beyond *all* their

8

struggles to make a better life, it was a pearl of greatest price.

It happened like this. Jack and Edward came to the bus stop one Monday morning – Edward with his hold-all and violin because he was now a weekly boarder at some music school, and Jack with his school bag full of messy homework – to find a girl waiting for the bus. Where she came from neither of them could imagine, for they lived out on vast and empty Whixall Moss, in a red-bricked house beside the lonely creek.

"Hello," said Edward, trying to be friendly.

Jack said nothing, just stared curiously.

The girl said nothing either, just stared across the Moss, towards the creek which in winter ran and ran, but now was beginning to go down. Her face was tired. She seemed fragile somehow, and her eyes were dark and sad and hard.

*What's the matter with you?* Jack wanted to ask, but he was too surprised to see her there and, in any case, the bus came along. The girl got on, and he lost the chance.

He had a busy day at school and the girl wasn't on the bus home, so he forgot about her until that evening, over supper.

"We've got neighbours, it seems," Mum said, trying to sound casual, but there was something in her voice; something which Jack recognized.

"Neighbours, where?" Dad said. Unlike Mum, who liked it out on the Moss all on their own, he liked people, and life, and things going on.

"On the creek," Mum said, nodding through the window, past the flower garden which was her pride and joy, and down the lawn.

"On the creek?" Dad said.

Mum tried to smile, but it wasn't easy. Her lips were drawn in too tight. "With all those miles of it to choose from," she said. "Right next to us."

After supper, she whisked Emily up to bed, and Dad went out to the workshop to get on with what he and Mum called "bringing in the money" – an important subject in their house. There was never much of it to go around, despite his hard work making furniture and Mum's fruit and vegetable market stall.

He seemed to have forgotten all about the neighbours. "Don't you want to come down the creek?" Jack said, who hadn't forgotten, most definitely. "Aren't you curious to know what Mum's on about?"

"Of course I am," Dad said. "But I've got to finish Uncle Pip's rocking-chair. He's been on at me. If you wait, I'll come down later."

Jack couldn't wait. It was Monday night, after all, and Edward had gone and the house seemed empty. He went alone, stalking through the orchard as quietly as a cat, and along the creek which buzzed with water-boatmen and dragonflies. Finally he found the neighbours, stuck almost out of sight behind the feather-fronds and roots of a row of weeping withy trees.

"That's what Mum's on about!" he thought, staring down among boggy reeds. "A canal-boat! Whatever's it doing in a place like this?"

The boat was long and narrow, had once been painted green, and quite obviously had seen better days. Its window boxes were empty and forlorn. The front of it was covered with a grubby old tarpaulin. The only sign of life was a bit of washing hanging on a line, and some thin smoke drifting up from a wonky tin-can chimney.

Jack stared at it curiously. It surely couldn't be a holiday boat – but then who would actually live on a thing like that? Suddenly he didn't feel so keen on neighbours nearby. He began to back off. It had always been their creek, but now he felt like a trespasser.

*Leave them to it*, he thought. But even as he thought it, something dogged and tenacious, which was always getting him into trouble, drew him back.

*Come on, Jack. Where's your sense of adventure?* the something said. *They'll be gone tomorrow, most probably. If you want to find*

11

*out why they're here and who they are, living in an old crate like that, now's your chance.*

The girl came on to the deck and unpegged the washing. The withies cast their evening shadows upon her, but Jack could still see her face. It was sad again – sad and cold. A light came on in the boat, and an electricity generator started up; he could hear it throbbing. A figure moved about inside.

Jack plucked up his courage. "Hello, again!" he called.

Maybe the girl didn't hear him. Certainly she didn't answer. She went in, banging a hatch door behind her. The sound of throbbing abated slightly. Someone drew the curtains.

She was at the bus stop the next day, this time carrying a shopping basket. The bus was late. They stood side by side in silence. Finally Jack plucked up the courage again, and said, "How long are you staying, then? Where do you come from?"

He tried to look friendly but the girl stared through him. She didn't answer and the silence grew. Jack began to wish that he hadn't asked. Then, suddenly, as if it was the last word on a subject which she'd been through and through, the girl sighed and said, "Dad and me are travellers. We don't come from anywhere. We move around, if you must know."

The bus came along, and she leapt on board,

sitting right behind the driver. Jack got on too, watching her from the seat at the back, trying to take in what she'd said.

*We move around, if you must know.*

He thought about it all day. Maybe she did live on an old crate, but for some reason it sounded exciting. Like a breath of fresh air blowing in upon their little creek, their little life. Not coming from anywhere. Not living as he did in a fixed place. But rolling on like the clouds in the sky. Having adventures. Being free.

"Have they gone yet?" Jack asked as soon as he got home from school.

"I think not," said Mum, who had been ironing sheets and was stacking them in a crisp pile. "Everything's quiet, but I'd swear I caught a whiff of burning peat from off the creek. You know what it's like. Nothing in the world smells quite like peat."

Jack did indeed know. Dad cut turfs of peat out of the moss and dried them in stacks behind the workshop, ready to burn at night.

While Mum began on supper, he went down the creek to investigate. Like Mum, he smelled the peat, and he saw the smoke from the tin-can chimney and thought, *If they don't move soon, the creek'll dry up and they'll be here all summer.*

The thought of it went through him. He

tried to imagine having neighbours all summer long – they who had always lived out here on their own – and part of him was fearful, but part of him was thrilled.

Edward returned on Friday night, handed over to Dad by his teacher at the bus station in town. The first thing Jack told him was about the boat, which he had been spying on all week, although he hadn't seen a soul.

"We ought to invite them round, if they're staying for a bit," he said. "Get to know them, don't you think?"

Edward liked his weekends back at home, quietly on their own. But he was always willing to go along with things. "Why not?" he said.

Jack brought it up at the end of supper. "All of us stuck here together," he said, hoping Mum wouldn't mind him putting it quite like that. "It seems a bit unfriendly if we don't try to get to know them."

Mum took away the plates. She didn't say anything. Dad looked at her, as if he wondered what she was thinking. Even Edward didn't say anything.

"Well?" Jack said, exasperated with them all.

"They probably want to be left alone," Mum said, returning to the table for the last few glasses. "I think we should leave things as they are."

It sounded pretty final, her *leave things as they are*. It went with her expression, which was fixed and tight. It sounded absolute.

And yet Jack couldn't help but try again, later when Dad came up to wish him and Edward goodnight. Edward was asleep already, but he was still awake – wide awake.

"I meant it about inviting them round. Please, Dad. I know what Mum said, but will you talk to her?"

At first Dad didn't answer, standing there in the dark. But then at last, he said, "Jack, are you very lonely here?"

Jack thought about it. There were things he liked about the Moss, but there were other things too.

"Yes, I'm lonely," he said

Dad looked down on him, his face so grave that Jack wondered what he'd said. "Of course it's no big deal," he hastened to reassure. "I just thought we could invite them round, that's all."

Dad smiled at him. There are moments that change everything. "And so we should," he said, as if he'd made up his mind about something. "Leave it to me. I'll talk to Mum."

# MIDSUMMER TIME

Next morning, Jack came down to find baby Emily crying in her pram, and Mum ignoring her while she finished off a letter.

"Take this round to the boat," she said, folding it in half. Her face was closed. Jack couldn't tell a thing from it. "Take it now."

She thrust the letter into his hand, and turned to get on with the breakfast, completely ignoring him any further. There was no sign of Dad anywhere. Jack had the distinct feeling that he was witnessing the tail end of an argument.

"I'll wait for Edward," he said. Edward was still busy with his morning's practice on the violin.

"You'll go now," Mum said coldly. "Take Emily with you, if you're *lonely*."

The word washed over Jack, like a cold wave. He grabbed the pram, feeling guilty.

Down the garden he hurried with it, and along the creek. As he went he read the letter, which issued a formal invitation to what Mum had chosen to call *Sunday afternoon tea*.

It sounded stiff and fussy, and not a bit like them, and certainly not what Jack had meant. He hurried along the creek imagining cakes, and awkwardness all round, and best china plates. He noticed how low the water was and almost hoped that the boat would have left while it could.

But when he reached the withies, it was still there, tucked almost out of view. He got up close, and a man was on his knees, poring over the engine. At first Jack couldn't see his face, just a mop of shaggy hair sticking out around his head. But then he lifted his head and Jack saw his eyes, tired and worn just like the girl's. Jack stared at him. Hair, face, eyes; everything about him was grey. And Jack had imagined that the travelling life was carefree!

"What are you staring at?" the man said.

"Mum sent me with this," Jack said, blushing and holding out the letter.

The man leaned over the boat and snatched it in a hand which was greasy halfway up to the elbow. He unfolded it and read it, while Jack waited and Emily started crying again. His expression was grim and unfriendly. Jack turned to lift Emily out of the pram but, before he could, the man thrust the letter back at him.

By now, it was covered in greasy fingermarks.

"I don't think so," the man said, without so much as a "thank you", or "it was nice of your mum", or "we would have liked to, but we're moving on". He waved his hand dismissively, looking so hostile and unfriendly that Jack grabbed the pram and began to twist it round on the towing-path, crying baby and all.

If the man wanted to get rid of them, then that was fine by him! He wished he hadn't come. He didn't like the dingy boat. He didn't like the man, who looked as if he'd never smiled in his whole life. The idea of his coming for tea – or of making friends with his cold-eyed daughter – seemed plainly ludicrous.

"All right, Emily, *all right*!" Jack said, wondering what he could have been thinking of. He yanked the pram violently – and Emily stopped crying, just like that. Every bit of her went still; eyes glassy, body frozen, mouth firmly shut.

Jack stared at the pram, horrified. For a terrible moment he thought he'd done something to Emily. It would be just like him. Always getting into trouble. Always doing dreadful things. Somewhere in the distance he heard a bird sing, like a soul ascending. *Oh, Emily,* he thought, and his heart pounded.

But then, as suddenly as she had frozen, Emily blinked. She opened her mouth in a silent gasp. Her eyes seemed to fix on something behind him, and her tiny body started trembling.

Jack spun around. Not only his heart, but every bit of him seemed now to be pounding. Emily let out a cry – and there, coming towards them between the trees, he saw…

He saw *what*?

Afterwards, he never could have said, exactly. All he knew was that hairs rose on his arms and on the back of his neck – and, on the boat behind him, the grey man drew in his breath.

"Who … who's that?" Jack said.

For an instant, even the birds in the sky seemed not to sing. Then, "It's only me," a voice said, and into view sauntered the girl.

She didn't say another word, just passed Jack by with a small, forced smile, and he watched her climb on to the boat, and he knew that he had caught a glimpse of something else between the withies. Something that disappeared as soon as it was seen, and was extraordinary and unbelievable and he couldn't take it in. He couldn't get his mind round it – but he had seen it.

Emily began to cry again and the moment passed. Jack grabbed the pram and ran. The last thing he heard was the grey man saying, "Are you all right?" and the girl replying, "Oh Dad, of course we are."

*We*, not I.

19

Jack thought about this all the way home, and on and off during the day, and even that night up in bed. Unless he was completely off his head, something remarkable had happened down at the creek this morning. He tried talking about it to Edward, but Edward wasn't curious like him. He made some fatuous remark about Jack fancying the girl, and Jack realized that if he wanted to find out more, he'd have to do it by himself.

Next morning he dressed and set off, leaving Edward to his Sunday morning sleep. The garden was fresh with dew; it was green and white with elderflowers and the first of the roses which Mum tended in the hope of producing the perfect flower. Jack walked between them and her tidy rows of vegetables; along the orchard, and out on to the creek, watching the swooping house martins, listening to a skylark sing, watching the sun on the water.

He wasn't frightened. Rather, he was curious. Nothing harmful could surely happen on a day like this; midsummer time when the nights were short and it somehow felt as though – with a little bit of luck, or if he held his breath or came up with the right wish – all the darkness in the world could be driven away.

Along the towing-path he trotted, savouring the beauty of the day. Moorhens paddled between the reeds, and a heron stood statuesque beside the water. Soon the boat appeared ahead, its curtains drawn; nobody awake yet – or so Jack thought. The world was golden. He passed under the withies.

And then he saw it.

Slipping quietly off the boat he saw it, down among the reeds and then up between the feather fronds of the withies, scattering diamond dew-drops as it padded out into the long grass and the buttercups. He saw what he had come for. But he wasn't prepared for it. How could he be?

How could anybody?

It was all too much. Astonished at himself, he began to cry. Never mind the beauty of the day, or the curiosity which had brought him here. On and on he cried. It must have been the shock. Even when he ran back home along the towing-path – away from the boat and away from it – he didn't think he'd ever stop.

# A GARDEN IN A SINGLE FLOWER

But of course he did stop, eventually. Everything stops, and in the end he got a grip on himself by deciding not even to *think* about what he might or might not have seen.

It seemed the best thing. Determinedly he didn't think about it all day. Through lunch he didn't think about it; through an afternoon in the garden, playing cricket with Dad, using Dad's worn old cricket bat; through a tea without visitors, and awkwardness and best plates.

Even next day, when he and Edward went off to their separate schools, doggedly Jack didn't think about it, telling himself that whatever it had been was due to the magic of high June, when you felt as if anything could happen. Surely it had been a midsummer daydream, and the memory of it would soon fade.

He longed for it to fade but, if anything, the

memory grew. It haunted his whole day, and he awoke the following morning to find that it had even haunted his sleep.

He got up. He had had enough. He had to do something, but he didn't know what. Edward's bed was empty. He couldn't tell him – and it was probably just as well, for Edward would have laughed at him. Nor could he tell Mum and Dad. They would think he was crazy. And perhaps he was.

He drew back the curtains, and it was wet outside – a heavy, sombre morning, unlike the magical one when anyone, he told himself, might have thought they'd seen something. The trees dripped, and the air was dull with grey rain. He began to dress. He would go back, he told himself. He would prove, once and for all, that he hadn't seen anything apart from sunlight through leaves, and early morning shadows. That when the girl came through the withies, she had been quite alone.

Off he set, comforting himself with the thought that there'd be no gold today out among the buttercups. Along the creek he hurried. Never mind his wet clothes and the fact that he'd forgotten his waterproof.

He reached the boat. The curtains were drawn, and there was not a sound within; not even the hum of the electricity generator. Rain rolled down the tarpaulin in a silver mist. Everything seemed wet and silent. He crept under the withies, crouching out of sight until all he could make out of the boat, tucked low among the reeds, was its tin-can chimney.

"Come on, wake up," he muttered. The withies were dripping on to him. He felt sodden and wretched, and was beginning to wonder what he was doing here. A strand of smoke rose from the chimney. *It would be warm inside,* he thought. Warm and dry.

At last the generator kicked into life, and a radio started up. The curtains drew back to reveal little squares of light. Bolts slid back, and the hatch opened. The man came on to the deck, followed by the girl. Jack watched them talk, out there in the rain.Then he watched the man go back in, and the girl make her way to the front of the boat.

She began to shake the water off the tarpaulin. She was quite alone, much to Jack's relief. The deck was empty, and the bank was too. Jack turned to go. He had seen enough. But then, from underneath the tarpaulin, he heard something.

The sound of it went through him. *No,* he thought. *No, surely not!*

But there it was again. Some sort of strange, deep whine.

"Hey! You be patient!" the girl said. She undid the tarpaulin and out from it bounded a beast with one, two, three, four, five, six heads.

24

Six heads.

*A beast with six heads*.

Jack had got it wrong about the magic of midsummer making him imagine things, and he had got it wrong about being crazy. He stared at the one body and the six heads. This was not a dream. He was seeing them as plain as day.

Somewhere a million miles away, the girl laughed. Jack had never heard her laugh before. She almost sounded like someone else, he thought, all the sadness and tiredness peeled away.

"Well, come on!" she said, patting one of the slender necks. "Let's go!"

She jumped off the boat, and the beast jumped after her, shaking the rain out of its coat and pelting out towards the Moss. There was gold on the creek after all, Jack thought. There were diamonds among the buttercups.

He watched the beast bound through mounds of bracken and out again, across long, dark channels where the peat had been cut, through a vast expanse of heather. With its silky, flying coat, long legs and six thrusting heads, it was an incredible sight. There were people who believed that strange things happened out on the Moss, but this was surely beyond even their wildest imaginings! Running in the rain, the beast was like an entire garden in a single flower, like a ballet in a single body, with never an ungracious gesture or a hint of toppling; one head now rummaging among the peat, another stretching up to a dripping birch tree, another shaking in the rain, another smelling the scents of morning, another searching for its friend, the girl, who was running after it, laughing again. Another turning back – and seeing Jack staring at it in astonishment.

For a brief instant, the head stared back. Even from a distance, Jack could see its bright blue eyes, glinting at him like finely cut jewels. Then – he couldn't think of any other way of putting it – then the eyes seemed to smile, as if his watching it was all right. The beast turned back into the long, wet grass, and the girl turned towards it, her face alive and bright – and Jack could quite see why. The beast was *fabulous*. In all his life, nothing had prepared him for a thing like this.

He stood beneath his tree, soaked to the skin but no longer caring. There are things you dream about – fabled lands with secret treasures, super-heroes, magic creatures that can talk and fly – and you want them to be true, you want to see them with your own eyes, but you know you won't.

At last the girl returned to the boat. She climbed on board, and the beast followed her. They both passed Jack close by, but the beast didn't look his way again.

"And about time too!" the girl's dad said, poking his head out of the hatch. "Look at the state of you both. You're soaked."

The girl scrambled out of her waterproof. She laughed. Her dad laughed. He sounded completely different to the grey man of the other day.

"Your breakfast's waiting," he said, throwing her up a towel.

The girl dried her face, and began to rub the beast's coat. Then the two of them followed the man down into the boat, and Jack heard the hatch shut and the bolts slide. A pang of envy shot through him. They were dry and warm inside their boat. Their breakfast was waiting for them, and their windows were full of light. Smoke rose from their chimney, and they had the beast. The beautiful beast.

He got up, cold and wet. For a few extraordinary moments, it had been a golden day, sunshine or not. But now it was dull again, and he felt lonely. Really lonely. He felt empty, and incredibly sad.

He went home. There was nothing to look at any more; no point in remaining. His dreams had come alive before his very eyes, and now they had gone. For the first time in his life, Jack felt poor. Never mind the crock of gold that Mum was always promising, compared with the girl and the grey man he had nothing. They had it all, not him.

A very passion of desire came over him, which he had never felt before. With his whole being, he wanted what they'd got. If only for a day, an hour, a minute, he wanted it to belong to him.

# BULLY BOY

Jack tackled the girl at the bus stop, where she waited as if it were her fate to keep bumping into him. It was still raining, and she was wrapped up in the waterproof again, hood over her head and only her hands on show, clutching a stack of shopping bags. *Could she be stocking up to leave,* Jack thought, *now that the creek was up a bit, thanks to the rain?*

It was too terrible even to think about. If this was the case, there was no time to waste. There were things, after all, that he had to know...

"Where did you get your *dog*?" he asked, shocked by his forthrightness, but out it came.

"I haven't got a dog," the girl said, in a hostile tone which discouraged conversation.

"You know what I mean," Jack said, edging towards her.

"I'm sure I don't," the girl said, and imperceptibly she turned away.

"I mean your *beast*," Jack said. "Your *creature*. Your *thing*. You know – six heads, six pairs of bright blue eyes, six necks."

The girl laughed. She glared at him with her cold eyes. "You're mad!" she exclaimed. But he could have sworn that she was frightened.

The bus came along and she hurried on board, sitting on the single seat again, right behind the driver. When he got off for school, she studiously looked away.

*That's it!* he thought, watching the bus pull out. *I made a mess of that. She'll be gone by tonight.*

He nearly didn't go to school – and he might as well not have done for all the time he spent worrying that now she would be on the return bus with her shopping bags full; now they would be casting off; now they would be gone, gone.

It was a complete surprise therefore, that when he got on to the bus at the end of the day, there she was, looking weary, shopping piled around her. His spirits rose. This was his chance to put things right! No questions, no hassle. He would just be *nice*...

"Let me help you," he said, when the bus pulled up on the side of the Moss. He even dared to pick up a bag – but the girl snatched it off him.

"Give that to me!"

Her voice sounded almost panicky. She

30

threw the bags off the bus, glaring at him as if he were a monster, to be got away from at all costs.

"I only want to help," Jack protested.

The girl began to stride along the peaty track which cut a black swathe through the Moss. He hurried after her.

"If you want to help, you can leave me alone," she said, looking desperately for another way to go.

But there was no other way to go, just the one, long, winding track – which Jack had as much right on as her, seeing as it was his way home.

"Couldn't we be friends?" he said. "I know I haven't exactly gone about things in the right way, but—"

"Just get away from me!" she burst out, breaking into a half-run.

"I only want to talk to you!" he cried, and something strange began to burn inside him, which he had never felt before – something which took hold of him and seemed to change him in some way.

The girl took a backward, frightened glance. As if she recognized something in him, she dropped her shopping and began to run, full-pelt out into the Moss.

"Hey wait! Come back! You'll get lost," Jack called, trying to sound as if he cared, but there was triumph in his voice; he was almost gloating. He had got her now! She didn't know the Moss like he did!

Abandoning his own bag, he began to run too. Through the bracken, over the heather, into the abandoned trenches where the peat had been cut and the undergrowth had come up again, over ground which was light and spongy on top and sodden underneath – shouting and chasing; not because he wanted to frighten the girl, but because there were things he had to know, and she was depriving him. She had it all, and she was depriving him.

All the while, up ahead, the girl charged on; quicker and lighter than he'd expected, almost as if she'd done this sort of thing before. The creek came into view, and the canal-boat low in the water. He could feel the girl's relief, rushing towards it single-mindedly. This was his last chance, he thought. He would catch her now, or not at all!

He forced himself on, lungs bursting, heart exploding. The gap between them began to close. He wrenched his ankle in a trench, and carried on, hardly noticing. They reached the withies. He plunged in amongst them, grabbing for the girl.

"I told you..." she gasped, panting, crying, twisting to get free of him, "there is *no dog*..."

"Whatever it is," he gasped back, shaking her in a sort of fury, "I've seen it. You can't fool me."

She didn't answer him. She didn't have to. The hatch on the boat flew back and the grey man appeared, brandishing a boat-hook.

"Get out of here!" he yelled, his hair sticking out, his face furious and pasty. "Who do you think you are, you bully boy?"

Jack let the girl go. The words hit him like a shock wave. Bully boy? Him? Suddenly, the something that had burned inside him faded clean away. He was himself again, panting and horrified, seeing himself through their eyes – a gaunt and gangling, big-eared, clod-footed boy, chasing a girl who was half his size.

"I'll kill you if you come back here!" the grey man yelled.

Jack hung his head. He didn't blame the man for what he said. The girl was on the boat now, flinging herself down through the hatch.

"I didn't mean..." he wanted to say. But what had he meant?

He turned and stumbled off, feeling worse than words can say. Between the withies, back into the Moss, away from the creek. When he arrived home later, he was limping on his wrenched ankle. His clothes were torn, he had lost a shoe and he couldn't remember where he'd dropped his school bag.

"Jack, not again!" his mother exclaimed, throwing down her gardening tools at the sight of him.

"The man on the canal-boat threatened to

kill me," he wanted to say by way of explanation. But what came out instead was: "It's incredible, Mum. You'll never believe it. I've seen a six-headed beast."

It was the only thing that mattered somehow.

Mum stared at him. Of course she didn't believe him. Her face set. "All right, Jack," she said, trying to keep a calm voice. "You'd better go inside and get out of those clothes."

He could have left it there, but he had seen this thing. He, not Edward, not any of them. Most certainly not Mum. The burning *something* returned. His voice shook.

"It's got six heads," he said, his voice ringing with pride. "It's got six necks and six pairs of the bluest eyes. You've never seen anything like it, Mum, in your whole life."

Mum's face flushed. "Really, Jack," she said. "Go inside, like I said, and get out of those clothes!"

Leaving her tools abandoned on the ground, she made for the house, leaving Jack alone. But even then he couldn't stop. Over and over he repeated the words incredulously to himself, like a litany.

"Six pairs of eyes. Six heads. It was incredible. I've seen a six-headed beast."

# GO QUICKLY – THIS IS YOUR CHANCE

By supper time, Jack had calmed down. He caught Mum looking at him once or twice, but she didn't say anything. After they had eaten, Dad said, "Jack. Dishes."

The two of them cleared the table and did the dishes together, then went outside, Jack still limping on his wonky ankle but insisting that it was all right. The evening was cool and quiet. To begin with they walked in silence. Flowers were falling off the elder trees, and the garden reeked with the scent of them. Bats circled the lawn, and an owl called from somewhere beyond the creek.

Jack wondered if the boat was still down there on the creek, or if the grey man had taken it away. It filled him with horror, the thought of him taking it away, and the beast being gone no sooner than he had found it.

"What's this you've been telling Mum?"

Dad broke in upon his anxious thoughts.

There was a weariness in his voice, as if he'd had enough of trouble between Mum and Jack. Poor Dad, Jack thought.

"It was nothing," he said. "I was mucking about. It was just a bit of fun."

"A bit of fun?" Dad said.

He looked at Jack searchingly and Jack knew – he could just tell – that Dad thought he'd made the whole thing up, not just for fun, but because Edward had his violin and he wanted to be special too.

He hung his head.

"Jack, if you've got anything, anything at all, that you want to talk about..."

They had always been so close. But Jack couldn't talk to Dad – not like this. He shook his head. "I'm sorry," he said.

That night in bed, what with the ankle, and what Dad had said and his empty reply, Jack could have cried. He tossed and turned, thinking that he could have made it all up, wanting Mum to be impressed with him, if it hadn't all been true. If he hadn't really seen a beast.

He thought about the beast – longing for it as if seeing it again would put everything all right. In the end, he decided to go down to the creek, ankle or no ankle. Only when he knew for sure that the boat was there and he hadn't driven it away, would he get any rest.

Downstairs he crept, wincing at every step,

and by the time he got into the kitchen it was plain that he wasn't going anywhere.

He put some milk on the stove, and sat in the darkness while it boiled. The light was on in the workshop. Through the window he could see Dad working, as he often did, late into the night. Every now and then a lock of hair fell over his eyes, and he'd wipe it away, carrying on, concentrating hard on doing what he could to "pay the bills and keep the bank manager at bay".

In the end, Jack made a couple of cocoas and took them in. Dad smiled and straightened up. The workshop was a mess of furniture and picture frames and odd little carvings which went down well in tourist shops. In the centre of them all was Uncle Pip's new rocking-chair, long overdue, but Dad had this way of going on and on at a thing until he got it right.

However, he was working on something else tonight.

"I'm making you a cricket bat," he said, lifting it up. "What do you think? It's time you had your own, instead of playing with my old thing."

Jack looked at the half-made bat, fashioned out of a piece of withy. Dad was trying to find an interest for him, something that he could be good at. Something that could be his alone, and would make him special in some way.

*Oh Dad!* he thought. He would have to tell

him, wouldn't he? They couldn't carry on like this.

"I wasn't mucking about," he said at last, sighing at the hopelessness of the task, but he had to try. "It wasn't just a bit of fun. I really did see a six-headed beast. Honestly."

Dad put aside the cricket bat, and sat down. He cradled his cup of cocoa, looking at Jack for what felt like the longest time. At last he said, "All right, Jack. Tell me about it. Where did you see this thing?"

Jack sat down facing him. He wanted to see his eyes.

"You're not just humouring me?" he pleaded. Desperately, he wanted Dad to believe him.

"Of course I'm humouring you," Dad said, with a gentle smile. "But anything is possible. You know I've always believed that."

Jack looked away. Perhaps Dad didn't quite believe him – but at least he was giving him a chance.

"Oh, Dad!" he said – and suddenly it all came out; about wanting to feel special, of course, just like Dad had thought, but that didn't alter anything, it had still been true; about feeling poor for the first time in his life, and chasing the girl, and not knowing what had burned inside him; even about crowing because he had seen the thing, not Mum, not Edward, not any of them.

But, most of all, out it came about the beast. How graceful it was. How beautiful and extraordinary.

"You've got to see it for yourself," Jack said. His eyes were shining.

"We'll go together in the morning," Dad said.

Jack returned happy to his bed – even though his ankle kept him awake long into the night. In the morning it looked bruised and puffy. He still wanted to go down to the creek more than anything, but he had to admit that something was seriously wrong.

"He's done it again!" Mum said to Dad, over breakfast. "He's broken something. I'll have to take him in after going to market. You haven't got the time. You've got to finish Pip's chair."

*Taking him in* meant visiting the accident and emergency department of the local hospital. This wasn't a big deal. They'd done it lots of times before.

"You need a season ticket," the nurse teased, when she saw Jack again. She was the one who'd stitched his thumb back on, and Jack had seen the X-ray lady twice before, and the doctor once.

"It's not a break this time," the doctor said. "But it is a serious sprain, all the same."

The nurse put an elastic bandage on his leg, which stretched from knee to toes, and hugged his ankle tight, taking away some of the pain.

"You'll have to keep him home from school," she told Mum, busy packing a crutch into the back of their car, along with the empty vegetable crates. "He shouldn't walk at all for a few days."

Mum's face was grim. "He's not very good at sitting around," she said.

The nurse smiled. "I can see that!"

When he got home, the first thing Jack wanted to know was whether Dad had been down to the creek, and the next was whether the boat was still there.

Dad ran his fingers through his mop of hair. "Uncle Pip phoned about his chair," he said, "and stupidly I told him it was finished. I'm sorry, Jack. Maybe later, when it is. Maybe after lunch."

Jack looked at Mum, rushing about the kitchen. It was no use asking her. She came across to him and almost pushed him down on the settee with a cushion under his leg.

"Don't move," she said. "Or else you'll make it worse."

It couldn't possibly be worse, Jack thought, stuck on the settee like this, watching Mum get him a lunch which he picked at when it came because he wasn't really hungry. Why did it always have to be like this? Mum always cross with him. Him always doing something wrong.

He fed his lunch to baby Emily, who was rolling round on the floor, desperate to walk – and he knew just how she felt. When his plate was empty, Mum whisked away the tray. Dad looked set to return to the workshop, and Jack tried again.

"You promised," he said. "About the boat."

"Later," Dad said, looking harassed. "I won't be long. Honestly."

Mum glared at Dad. *Now then. You be careful. Don't encourage the boy,* her look seemed to say.

Dad hurried away – and who could blame him? Jack would have hurried away himself, if he could have done.

When Dad had gone, Mum carried Emily out into the garden and laid her on a blanket in a shady spot. Then, crutch beneath her arm, she came back for Jack.

"You know what the nurse said. You've got to rest," she said, leading him to the orchard, where their big old hammock hung between the damson trees. "She also said to keep your ankle up – and that's exactly what you're going to do!"

She arranged the ankle cushion in the bottom of the hammock, helped Jack climb into it, and set the whole thing gently swaying. Then she left him to get on with her precious gardening.

Jack lay back. He had no choice, a prisoner beneath the damson leaves, staring at the sky and thinking furiously that there was more to life than gardening, and hammocks and Uncle Pip's rocking-chair! What was the matter with everybody? There were six-headed beasts with silky coats and shimmering blue eyes, and there were other things too, he had no doubt. He thought of what Dad had said. Anything is possible. Had he understood what he meant by that? *Probably not,* Jack thought.

He closed his eyes, hearing the bees hum among Mum's flowers, and the swooping house martins over the creek.

Perhaps he fell asleep. Certainly, when he opened his eyes, the day had changed. The sun had moved round and he lay in complete shade. His ankle cushion had somehow worked its way on to the ground and the hammock had stopped swaying. Dad's workshop door was open, and Jack could see the finally completed rocking-chair. There was no sign of Dad and, looking about the garden, there was no sign of Mum either, or of Emily. Perhaps the three of them had taken pity on him and nipped down to the creek. The idea was highly unlikely, but it was nice to imagine it – even though he could catch their voices and knew that they were really inside, having tea.

Suddenly, out of nowhere seemingly, the words *go quickly – this is your chance* came to him. He looked around. Where they had come from he didn't know. There was not a soul to see, and yet he knew that he hadn't imagined them. Even if they had come from inside his head, they had been *spoken*, not thought. He looked down. Beneath the hammock lay the crutch, and it came to him that all he had to do was tip out, careful not to land on his bad foot.

Jack hesitated only long enough to glance towards the house, checking that there was still not a soul to see. Then he rocked the hammock so violently that he couldn't help but fall out. For a moment he lay in agony, curled on the ground around his ankle, which felt huge and throbbing. Then, with a colossal act of will, he grabbed the crutch and made off.

"It's only an ankle," he told himself. "It's not a whole leg. There's nothing broken, nothing seriously wrong."

Across the orchard he hobbled, between the damson trees and through the long grass, driving himself towards the creek with only one thing on his mind, that he should find the boat and see the beast again.

He reached the water's edge feeling sick with pain. A heron rose into the sky, lifting its great wings and flying off. He stopped and watched it.

*It's not only six-headed beasts that are fabulous,* he thought. Maybe the pain had done something to him, or maybe it was the beast which, ever since he'd seen it, had somehow changed him, but certainly he'd never thought anything quite like that before.

He hurried on again, waiting for Mum to come shouting after him, but she didn't. Despite the pain he began to laugh. His shoulder ached from the dreadful crutch; his ankle was a dead weight. He still felt sick, and never had this walk along the creek taken such a long time. But suddenly he felt full of hope and excitement too. On he pressed. He could see the withies. He could see the reeds. He could see the place where the boat should be.

The *empty* place where the boat should be.

At last Jack stopped.

*The boat has gone*, he thought. *The whole thing is over*, and he stood there, feeling foolish for having tried, and bitterly disappointed and completely stuck. He couldn't go on. He couldn't go back. If he took another step, even his good ankle would give way under him.

He closed his eyes. He didn't know what to do.

# QUESTIONS

*Perhaps the beast had wanted them to be friends,* Jack thought later, when it was long-since too late. Perhaps it had wanted to rescue the girl from her loneliness, and it had seen the loneliness in him too and had tried to bring them together.

He would never know for sure, but what he did know was that as he stood there, eyes closed, he felt something close to him – as close as sunshine on a summer's day. And when he opened his eyes, there it was, its faces staring at him, each one so different – even though they shared the one body and the one life – each one so full of warmth and friendliness, each one so *beautiful*, that it took his breath away.

"You're real," gasped Jack, feeling stupid, but it was all that he could say.

The faces smiled at him. How did they do

that, smile like that? He didn't know. All he knew was that he found himself laughing in reply.

"You're real!" he laughed. "You're real. Look at you. I could even reach out and touch you."

His ankle stopped throbbing and his head felt clear. He wanted to shout out for the trees to hear, for the moorhens on the creek, for the heron who had flown away.

He began to dance for joy, throwing aside his crutch and wobbling on his ankle. The beast thrust out a paw to steady him. He clutched the paw. It felt soft, and he didn't want the moment ever to end, standing there like that, feeling the beast's warm life right there in his hand.

But at last the beast withdrew its paw and turned as if to move off. Not yet, Jack thought. The beast looked at him as if it knew what he was thinking. Its faces seemed to say, *Well, what are you waiting for?*

Leaving his crutch abandoned on the ground, Jack followed it. Along the creek they walked side by side, and so taken up was Jack with feeling like the king of the whole world, in a frenzy of happiness that he couldn't possibly have explained, that it took him a while to realize where they were going.

They were going to the boat – which hadn't gone, after all. Jack looked up and there it was.

Goodness knows why he hadn't noticed it before! The beast got down among the reeds and began to pad the last few steps towards it. Jack followed, mud squelching through his shoes, and this might have been the strangest thing that had ever happened out here on Whixall Moss, but if it was, he didn't care. He couldn't think about things like that. He couldn't be frightened.

He was beyond all that. Even when the beast leapt on board and he followed it, he wasn't frightened. So a man lived on this boat, who had threatened to kill him if he showed up again! What was that to him?

Jack was still lost in thought, shaking his head and wondering if this could all be happening to him, when the girl threw back the hatch and came on to the deck.

"It's you again!" she cried in consternation.

"I thought you'd gone," Jack said, remembering with shame the bully boy of yesterday. "I'm glad you haven't. I never would have forgiven myself if I'd frightened you away."

"We would have gone," the girl said, "but Dad had to take the engine off to be repaired."

"Then you're on your own?" Jack said.

The girl flushed and didn't answer. It was obvious that she wanted him to go. She looked towards the beast. Maybe she thought that it would protect her.

Jack looked towards it too, down at the

47

front of the boat, on the folded-up tarpaulin. He couldn't go, not yet. "What's it like, owning a thing like that?" he asked. He was desperate to know.

The girl shrugged. "My dad says there are some things you can never know about or really understand," she said. "All you can do is wonder at what they are."

Jack envied her. He really did. "You're so lucky," he said, and his voice was thick with longing.

The girl looked at him. "I wouldn't put it quite like that," she said, and there was a sadness in her voice, and the sadness was like a warning.

But Jack didn't heed the warning. "I'd be happy every moment of every day," he blundered on, "if only I owned a beast like that."

The girl laughed. Her expression was suddenly bitter. *What was wrong?* Jack thought. *What had he said?*

"Let me tell you something about being happy every minute of every day," she said at last. "Once we had friends, but not any more. Once we had a home, but not any more. Once we were ordinary people; we were a family, we lived an ordinary life – Dad had a job, and my sister Ruby and I went to school. Once we even had a mum. But not any more. Ruby has gone with Mum. Everything has gone."

Jack tried to understand. It sounded bleak;

it sounded horrible, her "everything has gone".

"You mean…?" he struggled.

"I mean you pay a high price to own a beast like that," the girl said. "People chase you, and you have to hide. They hound you, and you have to move on. They pester you night and day, and they don't mean to do it, but something always comes over them. They can't help themselves – even the best of them. I expect you know what I mean. Once you've seen the beast, there's only one thing on your mind. Isn't that right?"

Jack thought about his tossing and turning nights; about chasing her across the Moss; about burning inside. He knew what she meant, all right.

"Why don't you stay here?" he said, burning inside even now. "Never mind the past. You don't need to move this time. I won't pester you, and you've seen how lonely it is down here, and if anybody did come along, I'd protect you. Honestly. You can depend on me."

The girl looked at him, as if she knew that she couldn't depend on him, despite his "honestly". But there was a hunger in her eyes, all the same. Poor lonely girl! Jack felt ashamed.

"I sometimes even wonder about letting it go," she said, more to herself than anyone.

Jack shivered at the very thought of it. "If it were mine," he said. "I wouldn't ever let it go."

The girl smiled. "Oh, I think you would," she said. "If you could. If it would only let you."

She stared at Jack, and he shifted uncomfortably. She was telling him something, and he wasn't sure that he wanted to know. What he did want to know were the little, simple things, the safe things, like where the beast came from in the first place, and whether there were others of its kind, and if it had a name, and what sex it was and...

"There you are!" a voice broke in upon his tumbling thoughts.

Jack looked up, and along the creek came Dad, brandishing his crutch.

"You'd better get straight home before your mother finds you!" he called, looking none-too-pleased.

Get home? Not likely! Now was the chance which Jack had longed for all day. The chance to show Dad the beast – to prove to him that he hadn't made it up.

"Dad, oh Dad!" he cried, leaping off the boat and plunging recklessly towards him.

"Look out!" Dad cried – but Jack's ankle gave way under him, and he didn't even care, scrambling up again with only one thing on his mind.

"No, Dad. You look!"

Jack waved towards the boat, and Dad looked, sure enough. But the tarpaulin was deserted. The deck stood empty. There was nothing to see. The beast had gone.

Jack let out a cry. He began to stumble back towards the boat, calling on Dad to follow him. The beast must have crept into the cabin – either that or down among the reeds.

"Tell him," Jack shouted at the girl. "Get it out. Show him. Show me."

"Show you what?" the girl shouted back. There was a coldness in her face again. It was as if she had never spoken to him. As if they were strangers.

"You know what!" Jack cried, floundering among the reeds on an ankle that was killing him. "Show him the beast. Tell him that I didn't make it up. Tell him that I didn't imagine it."

The girl looked at Jack as though he was that bully boy again, who had chased her through the Moss. "I don't know what you mean," she said, and suddenly Jack was angry – more than angry. The something inside him not only burned; it raged.

"You know *exactly* what I mean!" he cried.

"Jack!" Dad exclaimed, leaping down among the reeds and shaking him. "Enough of this! You're coming home!"

He hauled Jack up on to the towing-path, and Jack raged at the girl, who had betrayed him, and at the beast, who had offered what felt like friendship, but had taken it away. Dad

51

dragged him home, and he raged all the way. He had well and truly lost his crutch technique, and Dad ended up carrying him, stiff and indignant, like an over-sized sack of potatoes.

Only when they reached the garden, did Dad put him down. Then he looked at Jack, and his eyes were full of sadness and kindness, all mixed up together.

"Well then," he said. "Tell me, are there others of its kind, or is it the only one?"

"Are there what?" Jack said. His heart went cold, for it might have worked in the middle of the night – something special out in the workshop between the two of them – but it was cruel to humour him now, cruel to pretend, after all he'd been through.

"Are there others of that … that thing of theirs?" Dad said, and his eyes were absolutely grave. "You know, that beast."

Jack stared at him. Something began to sink in. "Are you saying … do you mean … are you telling me…?" His voice petered out.

"Indeed I am," Dad said.

"You mean you saw it…?"

"Standing in the Moss," Dad said. "Watching us go."

# UNCLE PIP

There was no anger, only a terrible coldness when Jack came limping in, shoes split open, squeaking with mud, his stretch bandage smeared and halfway up his leg.

"That's it," Mum said, turning her back on him. "I've had enough. I wash my hands of him."

Jack grabbed her arm. "Oh, Mum," he said, desperate to put things right. "It doesn't matter. Mum, *please*. Listen to me. I've seen it again, and Dad has too. The six-headed beast. *We've* seen it."

Mum went from cold to hyperthermic in a second flat. She said, "What was that?" Then she looked at Dad and said, "No. Don't tell me. Don't say anything. I don't want to know."

Jack looked at Dad too, who shook his head. Jack realized that he'd chosen the wrong moment.

"Perhaps you could go upstairs," Dad said. "It might be better, Jack, just for now. Your mother and I will sort this out."

Jack limped up to his room and flung himself on to the bed. Downstairs, the arguing began.

"How could you?" Mum cried, as if she didn't care who heard. "You're such a fool! The last thing he needs is encouragement. I told you to be careful."

"I know you did!" Dad said. "But wait a minute, will you? Listen to me for just this once."

But Mum wasn't in the mood for listening. Jack heard her striding up and down. "What did I do to deserve a child like that?" she cried. "That's what I want to know. He breaks things, and he gets things wrong and he never learns. He's even got big ears – I mean look at him, look at his ears and look at those feet – and now he lies. He even tells lies."

She burst into tears. Jack closed his eyes and thrust his hands over his ears. He didn't want to hear it, Mum going on and on, and Dad really angry now; Jack had never heard him shout like that before. He was glad that he had the room to himself. He was glad that Edward was away at school.

He curled himself up into a tight little ball. The room was hot and fusty and he wished himself to sleep – wished himself anywhere but here. Downstairs, Mum was shouting now, and Dad was silent. Mum was almost screaming, and Jack could hear the slamming of the kitchen door…

It was the last thing he remembered, until he awoke to silence. At first it was a relief, that silence, but then as he lay there amid the shadows of approaching night, it came to him that it wasn't a peaceful silence somehow; it was brooding and ominous. He thought about the argument between Mum and Dad, remembering what the girl had said:

*Once we were ordinary people; we were a family, we lived an ordinary life. Once we even had a mum. But not any more.*

What had she meant by that? A dreadful fear came over Jack. He climbed off the bed and limped downstairs. The light was on over the kitchen table, and Mum was sitting at it, topping and tailing gooseberries ferociously.

"Where's Dad?" Jack said, unable to look into her red and swollen eyes.

Mum carried on topping and tailing. "He's out somewhere," she said. Her voice was hot and furious and weary. "He took the car."

Jack limped to the settee, and settled in the darkness between Dad's cricketing photographs and Mum's walnut piano with exotic cactuses lined along the top of it. He put his leg up on a cushion and tried to convince himself that it was an ordinary day. It was what he wanted more than anything. He picked up a book, flicked through the channels on the telly, tried to tell himself that everything was all right. A car came churning along the track. That'll be Dad, he thought, wishing him to come striding in, turning on the lights and laughing. He jumped up. By the time the car reached the house, he was at the door.

But it wasn't Dad, after all.

"We've got a visitor," he said, watching the car pull up.

"Oh, surely not!" Mum said, rising to her feet, her voice panicky.

The car lights went out. Its engine switched off and there was an instant of silence before someone leapt out, calling and waving and slamming the driver's door.

"You won't believe this, Mum," Jack began to say – but that was as far as he got before the whirlwind that was Uncle Pip bore down upon him.

"Jack, Jack, Jack!" Uncle Pip cried, overwhelming him in a great hug.

"Uncle Pip," Jack answered weakly.

"For all the times I've been here," exclaimed Uncle Pip, "do you know I *still* get lost out on those bloody peat tracks?"

He put Jack aside and swept on to Mum, his sister, who was as different to him as chalk to cheese. "Sorry it's so late," he declared. "You know why I'm here, of course. Is it true what he tells me? Has he *really* finished my rocking-chair?"

Mum took Uncle Pip in her arms. Usually she was pleased when he appeared, even though he turned her routines and her household upside down, but tonight she could manage only the thinnest smile, trying to look welcoming and yet obviously struggling.

"Is something wrong?" Uncle Pip said, holding her off at arm's length. His eyes were smiling, but there was something sharp in them that never, ever, missed a thing.

"Don't be silly, Pip," Mum said.

She moved away from him, and Jack watched her turning on the tap to fill the kettle. Even in their looks she and Uncle Pip were as different as people could be; she small and golden like Edward, and Uncle Pip dark and gaunt and tall. More like him.

Perhaps he was Uncle Pip over again. Perhaps that was what was wrong with him.

"You've been in the wars again, I see," Uncle Pip said, flinging himself down on the settee. "What happened to the leg?"

Embarrassed, Jack tried to brush it off, telling him that it wasn't as bad as it looked; it was only his ankle, and it was getting better anyway.

"That's the spirit!" said Uncle Pip. "No point fussing! Better to forget it, and get on with the next thing, that's what I always say."

Mum brought him a cup of tea. Would he like to eat, she wanted to know, and would he like to see his finished rocking-chair? Dad was out, but Jack would show him.

Uncle Pip looked at her quizzically. He drank down his tea in one go, and then he lit a cigarette. Yes, he would like to eat, he said, and he did want to see his chair. But first, he and Jack had business.

He winked at Jack. Jack knew what was coming next. "How are my four-leafed clovers shaping up?" Uncle Pip said, grinning.

Jack grinned too. He couldn't help himself, despite everything. The four-leafed clovers were sitting on the workshop window-ledge, a vital part of Uncle Pip's latest hare-brained, money making scheme: to propagate and sell what he called "lucky lawns". For every four-leaf bearing plant that Jack and Edward successfully dug up and transplanted, Uncle Pip had agreed to pay them fifty pence.

"So far we've found sixty," Jack said. "All of them seem to be surviving, you'll be pleased to know."

"*Sixty!*" Uncle Pip said, shocked because he plainly thought they'd dig up just a few.

"It's probably the peat," Jack said, unable to conceal his glee.

Even Mum almost smiled at that. "Thirty pounds you owe them, Pip!" she said, folding her arms.

"Good God, they'd better stop!" said Uncle Pip.

Jack burst out laughing. He wished that Dad was here to see Uncle Pip's face.

"A deal's a deal," Mum said – and he knew she'd hold Uncle Pip to every penny.

"A deal's a deal," Uncle Pip said, blanching. "Come on, Jack. You'd better show me my crop. For all this money, they'd better look good and healthy…"

Down to the workshop they went.

"They've been quarrelling, haven't they?" said Uncle Pip, as soon as they were out of earshot.

It was just like him. Once he'd latched on to something, he never let go.

"It's not like that," Jack hastened to reassure him. "Mum's tired, that's all."

Uncle Pip looked bullish. He knew that he was being fobbed off. "Well, what can she expect," he grumbled, "living out in a god-forsaken place like this? No shops, no neighbours, not even a proper road. Talk about making life hard on herself! I've told her and I've told her – but that's your mother! You can't tell her anything."

They reached the workshop. Jack opened the door. The lights were on, and the first thing they saw was the rocking-chair, varnished to the colour of honey. Immediately, Uncle Pip forgot everything else.

"I've never met anyone who can make a thing like your father," he said, rushing to admire it.

Jack knew what he meant. It might take a long time, but things were always perfect when Dad finished them.

Uncle Pip set the chair in motion, and you could see that he would have flung himself into it if the varnish hadn't still beeen slightly tacky.

Jack reached on to the window-ledge to get his clovers for him instead. But already Uncle Pip's darting, quicksilver eyes had hit on something else – the new cricket bat. He picked it up, turned it over, began to practise his strokes.

"All ready for the school team, eh Jack?"

"Not yet," Jack said. *Not ever*, he thought.

"When your father was a lad, he even used to practise in the snow," said Uncle Pip.

Jack could see a lecture looming on the subject of perseverance. "What do you think of your clovers?" he said, thrusting them deftly under Uncle Pip's nose. "There are sixty-one of them, but you can have the one for free."

Uncle Pip laughed. He said he'd go back indoors and find his wallet. They talked about clover propagation all the way back to the house, and he didn't mention Mum again, or say anything about quarrelling. But Jack knew that they hadn't heard the last of it.

Like the first breath of a storm, he knew that trouble was on the way. Even back indoors, with Uncle Pip chattering on and on, he could feel it coming. He watched Uncle Pip eating his supper, praising the rocking-chair, praising the clovers, even praising Edward and Jack for their business sense. But Uncle Pip didn't say a thing about his silent sister, who could hardly bring herself to look at him. He didn't ask her again what was wrong, and that in itself was ominous.

At last, Dad came in. Uncle Pip's face lit up.

"Here comes the man," he said, lighting another cigarette, "who can tell me why my sister's sulking. I want to know – is it something you've done, or is it me?"

Jack's heart sank. Here we go, he thought.

"Sulking?" Dad said, reeling at the sight of Uncle Pip.

"Of course I'm not sulking!" Mum said. But she didn't sound very convincing.

Uncle Pip laughed as if he had been waiting for this, and now he was enjoying it. "Oh yes you are," he said in that certain voice which he always saved for Mum. "You can't fool me. I'm your brother. I know."

Jack glanced at Mum. To his surprise, instead of laughing it off as she always did with Uncle Pip, she burst out with, "Don't you know when to leave a thing alone?" in a voice which was muffled and furious.

Uncle Pip stopped laughing. For a moment he blushed, as if he realized that unwittingly he'd gone too far. Then, with incredible smoothness, he launched into praising Dad for the rocking-chair, and laughing about the clovers, and telling them all about some other sure-fire scheme which he was in the middle of devising; why didn't Dad, who liked to, "chance his arm", come in with him?

He didn't say another thing about the sulking – but Jack knew that the storm wasn't over. Not that easily. Not yet.

Perhaps Mum knew it too. She glanced at the clock. Her face showed nothing, but when she said, "Jack. It's time you were in bed. You've had a long day," he realized that she was telling Uncle Pip that she had had a long day, too.

Jack hurried away. The last he heard was Uncle Pip picking up the cue and declaring that he really ought to go. Mum was going through the motions of saying that he was welcome to stay, and Dad was chipping in that it was a long way back so late at night.

Jack never heard how it finished up. He got into his own bed, and he hadn't been there long when Mum came in.

She asked after his ankle, staring down at him with her tired eyes. He knew that she had come up to put things right, in her own way. There were things she'd said that she regretted.

Things she knew he must have heard.

"It's feeling much better," he said, although the ankle still throbbed.

She tried to smile at him. "Let's start tomorrow with a clean slate," she said.

"A clean slate," Jack agreed, wishing that it could be that easy. If only Mum would just say sorry. But she wasn't like that.

When she had gone, he tried to get to sleep. The lights went out. He heard an owl across the creek. It called and called, and then it stopped and everything fell silent.

"Jack," a voice suddenly said.

Jack almost leapt out of the bed. The voice sounded close enough to have come from inside his head. Surely he wasn't hearing things for a second time that day?

He opened his eyes. And there, perched on the edge of the bed, was Uncle Pip.

"Help me here," he said, opening his wallet and counting out what he owed Jack in five pound notes. "You could do that much for me. We're chums after all, aren't we? And she is my sister – I care about what happens to her, you know. I've got it figured out as far as this. They've had an argument, and its probably to do with money. I mean that's life – it usually is. Perhaps your father's got some scheme of his own, and your mother doesn't approve of it. You know what she's like. Perhaps he's already had a go and it hasn't worked out, or there aren't any jobs coming in, or the market stall is failing." He paused and looked at Jack, but Jack didn't say anything. "But then, of course," he carried on, "it could be more than that. I don't know what, but it could be really serious. They could need someone to help them. Are you with me, Jack?"

Jack was with him, all right. Uncle Pip would go on and on until he knew everything. He, Jack, had to stop him. "I really don't..." he began to say, but Uncle Pip interrupted.

"Oh, yes you do," he said. "You know exactly what I'm talking about. Come on Jack, have a heart. What's going on here? Why so secretive? You've never kept secrets from your old Uncle Pip."

*That's what you think!* Jack thought, glad that in the dark his uncle couldn't see him blush. He took a deep breath. "Nothing's going on," he said. "Honestly."

Hardly surprisingly, Uncle Pip didn't believe him. "Oh, I think it is," he said. His voice was cool. He even began to fold up the money as if he didn't intend to pay it. "But you're not going to tell me, are you, Jack?"

Jack looked at Uncle Pip; now getting to his feet, now standing over him. He wasn't bad, not really, but he always had to know things.

"You're right, I'm not," said Jack, who could be bullish too.

Uncle Pip smiled. Too late, Jack realized

that he had admitted something with his "I'm not". It wasn't much, but Uncle Pip put the wad of money back on the bed.

"Oh, I nearly forgot. For your clovers," he said.

# *BETRAYAL*

Jack lay awake into the night, completely exhausted and yet feeling as if he'd never sleep again. The trouble was that he knew Uncle Pip, and what he was capable of. He may have given something away when he said "I'm not," but he would get no peace in return. Uncle Pip would go on and on until he knew all about the beast.

Jack shivered at the thought of it. This was certainly going to beat lucky lawns! He imagined Uncle Pip marching down to the boat and demanding to know what the beast was called, what it ate, what sort of noises it made, how it would propagate. He imagined Uncle Pip demanding to see the beast, and the grey man fighting him off, and the boat disappearing down the creek never to come back again.

In the end, goodness knows how, Jack fell asleep. But even there he found no peace, for he even dreamed about the beast. It was changing everything. Like a light, it was revealing things: Mum in a grief which Jack didn't understand, Uncle Pip in a dogged curiosity which lay like bedrock beneath his friendliness, Dad in an anger which he had never shown before. It even revealed him, Jack, in what he felt about a world which was all right on the surface but was something else beneath. A world of failure and big feet.

He woke up suddenly. It was dark in his bedroom – dark and hot. He got out of bed. His whole body was trembling. He got dressed. Without asking himself what he was doing, or why, he crept downstairs. Past the bulk of Uncle Pip asleep on the settee, and outside to the garden.

Here the air was soft and fresh. The sky was bright with moon. Down the lawn he walked, even though his ankle was still aching, past Mum's flower garden, her roses white in the moon, past her beans and peas and onions in their rows, through the orchard and down to the creek, where the silence was broken only by rustling leaves and lapping water.

Soon the withies were in sight, and the boat tucked tight among the reeds, its curtains drawn. Jack crept towards it. Suddenly his trembling left him and he felt calm. Even his ankle didn't bother him any more. This was what he had woken up for, he thought. This was why he had got dressed. To sit by the boat and guard it in the night. To keep it safe from Uncle Pip right through until morning.

He settled astride an old root, peering at the curtains and imagining the beast behind them. Was it asleep, he wondered? Surely it should sleep in splendour, on a bed fit for a king. In the moonlight, the boat seemed an unlikely house for a king. Its flower-boxes looked more than empty; they looked dead. Its peeled paint hung dull and grey. No smoke came out of its tin-can chimney, nor did its generator hum.

It must have been a nice boat once, Jack thought, but now it looked as if it hadn't been lived in for years.

Suddenly the hatch door opened and the girl appeared. Perhaps he had willed her to, or perhaps she couldn't sleep either. At any rate, she scrambled over the roof of the cabin to the tarpaulin. The moon shone on her hair, and on the huge white jumper which came down to her knees. But Jack hardly noticed what she looked like, for she undid the tarpaulin and the beast came leaping out.

Over the cabin roof it leapt and along the deck, and the sight of it, silver and moon-struck, made Jack forget everything else. He watched it leap off the boat and bound through the reeds. He could have watched it for ever. The girl came running after it, but he hardly noticed her until she ran into him.

"You again!" she exclaimed, drawing back, shocked, from this strange boy who was sometimes nice, but sometimes had to be dragged off screaming.

"Can't keep away," Jack said, trying to make light of the thing.

"So I see," the girl said, and Jack waited for her to shout for her dad; he braced himself. But she smiled instead. Actually *smiled* at him. Maybe the moonlight was doing something.

Maybe it was doing it to both of them. Jack scrambled to his feet, heart thumping. "Look, I'm sorry about yesterday," he said, with a sincerity that rang out and quite astonished him. "I don't know what came over me. Can I walk with you? I promise I'll behave. I really mean it this time."

The girl looked at him as if she could tell that he'd never meant anything so much in his whole life. "If you like," she said, and she smiled again.

Jack grabbed his chance and followed her out into the Moss. Suddenly the world was different from what it had been before. It was a different life, a different Moss. Walking by her side, he had never felt like this before. For some reason he remembered Dad saying, "Are you very lonely here?" and him replying, "Yes, I'm lonely – but it's no big deal."

But it *had* been a big deal, he could see that now, and it was a big deal still. He watched the beast run ahead of them, shining, leaping, bounding. He didn't ever want to be lonely again. He didn't ever want to let the beast go.

"Do you ever get used to it?" he asked.

The girl shook her head. "No, never," she said.

They walked past turfs that had been cut out of the moss and were stacked up high; over heather; across deep, dark, lichen-covered waterways; through a swaying sea of grass. Jack savoured each moment, savoured the night, which was passing. In the eastern sky, he could already see the first hint of day.

"Even your ankle is better," the girl said, watching him walk without a hint of hobbling.

Jack didn't answer. His ankle was the last thing on his mind, for they were nearly back where they'd started and the withies waited ahead of them – pools of shade within the deeper shade of night. They made a good place for the boat to hide, but there was something about them which Jack had never noticed before. Something which made him feel uncomfortable. Like a row of sentinels they were, standing between him and his old life. Maybe he didn't want to go back to that old life. Maybe he wanted to stay this side of it, out in the moonlight.

"I don't even know your name," he said, drawing back.

The girl drew back too. She turned towards

him. Later he was to remember the moment so clearly. "Names aren't what's important..." she began to say. But Jack couldn't take it in. He couldn't concentrate. Out of the corner of his eye he could see the beast beneath the withies. It hadn't drawn back like him. It was entering their darkness.

He let out a cry. He didn't know why.

And his cry ... his cry was *answered*.

The girl broke off. Jack stared in horror as the withies shook and the beast came running towards them, its heads down and bobbing, its ears pinned back, its coat sleek and streaming. He stared in horror as running after it, in hot pursuit, came Uncle Pip.

*Old Uncle Pip!*

Jack watched him race through the grass on wild man's legs. He should have stayed by the boat, he thought. This was all his fault. He had led them into this. He must have known, deep down inside, that Uncle Pip would follow him.

His hands knotted tightly into two hard fists. "*Stop it. No! Uncle Pip!*" he yelled.

The girl stared at him for a moment, her face full of shock and blame, then she turned away from him. She stumbled for the boat, and the beast ran beside her, and Uncle Pip ran after them.

"*No, no, no!*" Jack cried.

He began to run too, but it made no difference what he did. The thing was over. It was

71

over. There was even light in the sky – an ugly morning light which had arrived at last to drive away the silver night.

At last Jack caught up with Uncle Pip. He shouted in his face, "Stop it, stop, stop!" He even tried to haul him back along the towing-path. But Uncle Pip was beside himself. He was a big man, and Jack was easily shaken off.

*I'll kill you*, Jack thought.

But he never got the chance.

The girl reached the boat. The grey man appeared, clutching his boat-hook. The beast leapt on board and Uncle Pip made to follow it.

"That's as far as you go!" the grey man yelled, like an avenging angel with a voice of death. He swung the boat-hook – and for the first time Uncle Pip seemed to realize what he had got himself into. He stepped back, but it wasn't enough for the grey man, who advanced on him.

"No harm intended, no harm intended," Uncle Pip said. His face blanched, and his voice came out thin and reedy. Jack had never heard him sound like that.

"Get out of here!" the man yelled, in a voice which was tough enough to crush rocks. Again he swung the boat-hook over his head.

Uncle Pip got the message. He turned and fled – and Jack would have fled too, if he hadn't been rooted by terror to the spot.

The grey man turned on him.

"Dad, no! Dad, come on!" the girl called. She sounded desperate, hurling herself off the boat and pulling at the man who, much to Jack's relief, seemed to come to himself, and realize what he was doing.

He dropped the boat-hook. He and the girl climbed back on board. She hid the beast under the tarpaulin. He began to crank the engine into life, moving automatically as if this was something they had done before. The girl untied the mooring ropes and leapt up by his side.

"I'm sorry," Jack shouted from the bank. "Really I am. I didn't mean to betray you."

The girl didn't even glance at him. She was too busy. They both were. The engine was roaring – smoke pouring out of it, pungent and gassy – but the boat wouldn't move. Even when a venomous blue cloud stretched right out across the reeds, it wouldn't move. The creek was too low. The boat was stuck fast.

The grey man jumped out again, clutching the boat-hook which he began to dig underneath the boat, pushing and pushing. Jack took his life in his hands and leapt down among the reeds to join him. The girl was at the tiller. Still neither of them looked at him. The grey man tried the boat-hook under the other side of the boat. He pushed, and Jack pushed too, wanting to do something, wanting to prove that this was not his fault. That he was on their side.

The boat moved slowly at first, but then at last it drifted out towards the middle of the creek. The man leapt on board, helped up by the girl. They were right out in the middle now, where the water flowed. Still neither of them looked at Jack as it carried them away.

# KNOTWEED

It took Jack a long time to walk home along the empty creek, slowly, slowly, passing Uncle Pip's trail of havoc on the way; withy fronds torn, Moss trampled underfoot, the bottom plank of the garden fence smashed as if Uncle Pip had careered into it in his panic.

Jack walked up the lawn. Even Mum's flower garden had not been spared, blooms down and flowers torn. The only consolation was that the drive was empty where Uncle Pip's car had been. At least Jack wouldn't have to face him. He hoped Mum had sent him packing.

He went inside. Mum was quietly folding up the settee-bed. Her face was grim. He leaned against the door. She didn't say anything, just looked past him to where her roses lay, cultivated for a perfection which they would never now achieve. She seemed stunned.

"I'm really sorry, Mum," Jack said.

Mum looked at him at last. Her eyes were cold. Her voice was cold, too. She didn't say anything about the flowers. Instead she said, "Your uncle tells me he's seen a six-headed beast."

The words went through Jack. "Oh, Mum," he said. "It's so *beautiful*. Why won't you believe it?"

Mum looked away again. There was a bitterness in her eyes which Jack had never seen before. She didn't answer him, just said, "Your uncle says I used to sparkle, but I don't any more. He says I used to have vision, but it's all gone."

Jack looked at her skin, weathered by the sun, and her worn eyes and nut-brown hair flecked with grey. He couldn't imagine her ever having sparkled, but he supposed she must have done. Nor did he know what Uncle Pip meant by *vision*. Not exactly. But whatever it was, it had hurt Mum.

"Don't you worry about Uncle Pip," he said. "He's got it all wrong. Ask anyone. You're full of vision."

"Show me your beast," Mum said. "Then I'll believe you."

Jack stared at the settee-bed, all folded up. It was so unfair. She had asked too late.

"The beast's gone," he said.

Mum laughed, as if she hadn't really meant

it. "There it is," she said. "The beast's gone, Pip's gone – even my flowers have gone."

"What's that?" Dad said, coming downstairs in his dressing-gown, tousled and half-awake. "What's gone?"

Jack began to tell him about Uncle Pip, but as the story unfolded, Mum got up and walked outside, past her trampled flowers, down the path and on to the empty Moss.

Dad stopped Jack. "Later," he said.

Later Jack said, "Why won't Mum believe it? I mean we've *seen* the thing."

Dad sighed and said, "Who can say? She didn't used to be like this. You've heard her yourself, Jack – she used to think that if she worked for it she'd find the crock of gold at the end of the rainbow. Pip's right you know. She *has* lost her vision."

Jack went outside and began to pick up the flowers. The torn ones he brought inside and put in a vase, the others he tied back. All the while, he thought about Mum's vision which, like the beast, had gone. What did it mean to have a vision? And why had it gone? He didn't know.

In the end, Mum came along. For a while she stood watching him, then, without a word, she went and picked all her choicest things – fresh potatoes with the thinnest skins, tiny broad beans in cushioned pods, sweet smelling raspberries – and took them into the house and made a special lunch.

It was as if she wanted, more than anything, to put things right. Jack sat between her and Dad, smiling at them both, wanting things to be right, too. But, deep inside, his heart grieved. It couldn't stop.

It grieved about all sorts of things; the sadness in Dad, and the vision that had gone out of Mum, the boat that had gone, the girl who once had a home but not any more – even that Jack had never found out her name.

But most of all, his heart grieved about the beast.

It was so unfair, Jack thought again. He had loved that beast – quite simply, he had loved it – and now all he had was the memory of it running through the Moss, the memory of its faces looking up at him, and of its blue eyes.

*What good were memories?* Jack thought. They were bits of cardboard. They didn't live. They didn't breathe.

He went down into the workshop, for no other reason than to get away and be alone. Where else could he go? If he walked into the Moss he would see the beast. If he walked beside the creek, he would see it.

The workshop was packed with all sorts of things, including Uncle Pip's rocking-chair, which he had left behind, and the clovers on the window-ledge. Jack thought about the money laid out on the counterpane. Thirty pounds it had been! *Thirty pounds*, and Uncle Pip had left the clovers behind, forgotten in his excitement over some new thing! That was typical of him.

Dad came in. "I suppose we'll have to take them to him," he said, looking at the clovers and the rocking-chair. "But not yet. Not for a while. Let's forget him just for now. Let's go out and forget everything."

It was as if he knew exactly how trapped and wretched Jack felt. He went and got out the car. Mum gave them a shopping list, reminding them to pick up Edward from the station on their way home. She didn't ask where they were going or what they would do, and they didn't tell her. They couldn't have done. All they knew was that they wanted somewhere quiet, on their own.

Off they drove, along the Moss, bumping up and down. Jack thought about the way that people in town laughed, and said that there was something strange about Whixall Moss. *If only they knew*. A shiver ran through him.

They reached an inlet in the creek with a little beach. Dad pulled up, and they sat in silence. Jack knew that whatever Dad might have said about forgetting things, they couldn't really.

"Let's get out," Dad said, at last.

His voice was casual, but Jack knew exactly

what he hoped they'd find. They got out of the car. Jack was hoping for it too. They had to be out there somewhere, the grey man and the girl. They couldn't have got *that* far.

He walked to the water's edge. Something burned in him again, like a long-lost friend come back to haunt him. His heart pounded. Would he see the boat, tucked out of sight? Would he see the beast?

The inlet was empty.

"Let's try further on," Dad said, disappointment in his voice.

He didn't say what they were trying for, and he didn't have to. Jack knew that whatever burned in him, it burned in Dad too.

They got into the car and drove on. Along the whole length of the creek, faster and faster, stopping again and again, but there was never anything to see.

On they carried all the same, driven by an unspoken sense of mission, along a network of peat tracks, never giving up; in and out of the bog, up and down the entire vast and lonely Moss, emerging on to banks which were still always empty. There was never anything to see.

Finally, they reached the place where the creek joined the big river. They got out of the car. Houses stood in front of them, and proper roads and the whole wide waterway – another world completely from their quiet creek, with its dips and inlets and its lovely withies.

"If they've gone beyond this point, we'll never find them," Dad said, staring as sail boats and holiday cruisers passed by.

"Perhaps they haven't, though," Jack said, remembering the blue smoke and juddering engine. "Perhaps they've broken down somewhere."

They looked back along the creek. "Where are they, then?" Dad said.

Jack shrugged. They had looked everywhere. He didn't know. It was getting late.

"Mum'll be wondering where we are," Dad said, like a man waking from a dream, seeing all the places it had taken him. "We've been out all afternoon. We ought to go home."

Neither of them wanted to, but they drove home, stopping once or twice on the way, but it didn't feel like a mission any more; it felt like an army retreating. And when they got home, far from wondering where they were, Mum was furious. Never mind that they had forgotten about her shopping list; they had forgotten Edward, waiting for them at the bus station!

Dad tried to apologize, but there was really nothing that he could say. "How *could* you both?" Mum cried. "He phoned over an hour ago. What can you have been thinking of?"

Dad drove off fast, leaving Jack to follow Mum about the house, trying to put things right. She stormed about her dreadful afternoon:

81

Emily crying all the time because she could nearly walk but not quite, and some stupid problem with the stove, and some other problem down among the awful knotweed, which Mum rued the day she'd planted.

Jack followed her into the garden. There was none of her wanting any more to put things right. He watched her stuff Emily's toys into a baby blanket and stomp indoors with them. He followed her back into the kitchen, and there she stood in the middle of the floor, looking lost, her face as white as death, looking as if she didn't know what to do with herself. She just didn't know.

*What was the matter with her?* Jack thought. It was surely more than just their forgetting Edward.

Upstairs in her cot, Emily started to cry. But Mum didn't seem to notice her.

"Mum, what *is* it?" Jack said. He went and poured a drink. Not her usual cup of tea, but a glass of whisky.

Mum took the whisky, but she didn't drink it. Like Emily's crying, she didn't even seem to notice it. Jack looked into her face, and there was something in it. He could almost see it. It was as if they were on the border between their own safe world and another one.

"Tell me what happened," he said.

Mum looked at him. "No, you tell me," she said, and her face was grim. "Right from the beginning. Tell me."

Upstairs, mercifully, Emily fell quiet. Jack told Mum everything. She walked up and down and began to sip her whisky. He started with the girl at the bus stop and finished with the pool of shade under the withies where Uncle Pip had hidden, and then sprung out.

By the time he'd finished, it was getting dark. He told Mum how they'd searched and searched but the boat had gone.

She finished off the whisky. A ghost of a smile flickered across her mouth. Jack couldn't imagine why, but he was relieved to see it, all the same. Perhaps Mum was going to be all right.

She went to the sink and rinsed out her glass. "I wouldn't worry about them being *quite* gone," she said at last.

Jack was always to remember the tap running, and her turning it off. "What do you mean?" he said.

She nodded down the garden. "They must have done this sort of thing before," she said. "They're very clever. They're where you'd never think to look. Not down the creek, but almost where they started. Hiding in our knotweed."

# AS IF IT NEVER WAS

Before Jack could say a thing, their car pulled up outside and Edward came bursting out of it, complete with his week's news and a bag of dirty washing which he wanted Mum to do.

"Have you seen my grey jumper, I can't find it anywhere at school? Have you saved some supper? You'll never guess what…"

Mum took the washing in silence, and Edward rushed through the house as he did every week, to check that nothing had changed and to reclaim his room.

"Tell me again," Jack said, the moment he had gone. "Tell me where the boat is."

"It's under the Chinese knotweed," Mum said in a low voice, as if imparting some dire secret. "You know what it's like down there – an excellent place to hide."

Jack did indeed know. The Chinese knotweed was a terrible thing, growing like the furies.

"However did you find them?" he asked, imagining the boat tucked down there out of sight.

Mum looked at him. Her face was strange, and suddenly he felt strange too. He felt cold from head to toe. He didn't need to ask. He knew.

"Mum, you've seen it, haven't you?"

Mum looked away. Before she could answer him, Edward came bursting in demanding supper, and Dad appeared too, and they all sat down.

Jack sat down too. He could hardly contain himself. Mum had seen the beast. She had seen it for herself!

He wanted to tell Dad straight away, but the look on Mum's face held him back. She gave him his supper, and he tried to eat it. Edward started on about their forgetting him, and what Mrs James had said, who had had to wait with him. He didn't seem to realize that none of them were listening, Jack looking at Mum, and Dad looking at Jack, and Mum thinking her private thoughts and pushing her food around her plate.

*Please,* Jack's eyes said, and *Don't you dare!* Mum's eyes said back, and *What's going on?* Dad's eyes wanted to know.

"Is something wrong?" Edward asked at last.

Mum glared at Jack, but he couldn't keep it

in. "You're never going to believe this…" he began.

But before he could get any further, someone knocked on the kitchen door.

Mum looked relieved. Dad got up to see who it was. Jack could have wept with sheer frustration.

"Tell them to go away," he cried. Never mind who it was, or why they might be thundering on the door!

Dad opened up. Before he could say a thing, the grey man came bursting in, his face distraught, his eyes burning round at them all.

"Where is it?" he cried furiously. "Come on, I know you've got it. You can't fool me!"

They stared at him. What a meal this was turning out to be! The man's eyes settled on Jack, as if he was the source of all his troubles.

"I haven't got it!" Jack half rose, remembering the way the man had swung that boat-hook. "Honestly. Don't look at me."

"Got what?" cried Edward. "What's everybody on about?"

"The six-headed beast, of course," Jack said. Edward gawped. The man turned his attention on him. "How about you?" he said, in a voice which was thick and threatening.

Edward blanched. Here he was, a perfectly ordinary boy, and he had returned home to a madhouse! "I don't know what you're on about!" he cried in a little voice that shook.

Mum hurried to his side, looking daggers at the man. The man stepped back. For the first time he seemed to realize what he was doing.

"Have you seen my beast?" he said. "That's all I want to know. Just tell me and I'll go."

His face was terrible. "Why do you want to know?" Jack said.

But it was obvious.

"Because it's gone," the man said.

Jack couldn't help but pity him. "*Gone?*" he said. His stomach lurched at the thought of it.

"As if it never was," the man said. "As if it never had existed."

For a moment, the two of them stared at each other. Then the man turned away, and he wasn't shouting any more. It was as if the words he'd spoken had diminished him. As if they were too much for him. Out into the night he stumbled, unable to bear their presence any more. Whatever happened next, you could see that he was defeated.

# A PERFECT DAY

It was Emily who found the beast, not Jack or any of the rest of them. It happened this way. Jack awoke late next morning, hardly surprisingly. It had been a long night, what with all the sitting up and talking, and the hunting down the creek, calling and calling but to no avail. He drew back the curtains, and there was Emily, out in the garden on her blanket, playing with her toys and singing a little song.

Mum was in the kitchen. No getting up late for her, whatever time she went to bed! Jack could hear her moving about while the washing machine churned, and saw her going out to the line with a basket full of Edward's wet school clothes. Dad was in his workshop, the door open and Edward in there with him; Jack could hear them talking.

The sound of Emily's singing floated between them all, drawing them together somehow. It was like the morning's calm after last night's storm. Across the garden it carried, down to the creek, into the workshop, through the windows of the house and up to Jack.

*Oh, Emily!* he thought, and he hoped that the people in the boat could hear it too, and it would comfort them. He leaned against the glass, thinking how sweet his sister was, and how glad he was that they had her.

He closed his eyes. Maybe he even dropped off momentarily, but certainly the next thing he noticed was that the singing had stopped.

He waited for it to start again, as it surely would because once Emily got going, there was no end to it. However, the moment had passed apparently, and he got up from the window, feeling sorry. It was only by accident, reaching for his jeans across the back of a chair, that he happened to glance outside again.

*No wonder Emily isn't singing!* he thought. *Look at her!*

Somehow she had got herself upright on the blanket, and was standing wobbling on her little legs. *She's going to do it!* Jack thought. *She's actually going to walk,* and he leant out of the window for a better view.

He got a better view, all right – but it wasn't quite what he'd expected! Nor was it what Mum expected, who came out with another pile of washing in her arms. Nor was it what

89

Edward expected, who came across to the workshop door. Nor was it what Dad expected, who followed him, their conversation cut off mid-sentence.

They all gasped.

Emily walked across the blanket – one step, two steps, three. She walked out on to the grass, and they gasped again and it wasn't that she was walking, who had never walked before. Rather, it was that she walked to – the six-headed beast!

Emily reached it, and her legs gave way. She sat down hard, and the beast lowered one of its heads to check that she was all right. It even pawed her curiously, as if it had never seen a baby before. Emily took the paw in her tiny hand, and standing at his window, Jack knew exactly how she felt. The beast lowered its other heads, surrounding Emily with them, and she laughed, and Jack knew what that felt like too, laughing like that and never wanting the moment to end.

Extraordinarily, Mum didn't rush to protect her baby. And when Edward made towards Emily, she actually moved to stop him. "Not yet," her hand across him seemed to say. "This is Emily's time."

And, as if she knew it, Emily began to sing again. Louder and louder she sang. On and on. Jack thought she'd never stop. More than ever, it felt as though they were being drawn together. Drawn by what they heard, but also drawn by what they could see, standing there in front of them; beautiful and astonishing.

Only when Emily finally stopped, did Mum cross the lawn. The beast watched her. Mum picked up Emily.

"That was brilliant. Well done," she said, in an attempt at a brisk, no-nonsense voice. "But now it's time for breakfast, Emily. Your friend can come with you if he, er, she, er, it, wants to."

She turned away and, as if it understood, the beast began to follow her towards the house. Jack hurried downstairs in time to see it entering the kitchen. Mum put Emily in her highchair. Dad and Edward came in.

Mum brought out the breakfast and they all sat round the table, trying to act normally and not to startle the beast. But, hardly surprisingly they couldn't eat.

Far from being startled, the beast lay sprawled across the floor, its heads resting between its paws. Jack glanced at Mum. Her coffee had gone cold, and he wondered what she was thinking. He watched Emily trying unsuccessfully to feed the beast with unwanted bacon and fried bread.

At last Dad said, "Someone's got to tell them, down on the creek."

He got up, pushed aside his plate. He didn't sound as if he wanted to, and anyone but Dad,

Jack thought, would have kept the beast and never let on.

"I'll come with you," Jack said, feeling unaccountably proud of him.

They walked down the garden to the jungle of knotweed. The boat looked just as uninhabited as it had done the other night. Jack imagined the grey man jumping out on him again, with his burning eyes and metal boathook. He was glad of Dad's company.

"Is anybody home?" Dad called, when they got close enough.

There was no reply.

Dad climbed on to the boat and Jack followed in his shadow. The curtains were drawn and the hatch was shut. Through a crack in it, Jack made out the cabin which was long, narrow and empty, apart from dirty dishes, unmade bunk beds, a cold black stove and a pile of forlorn-looking books, stacked on a couple of dusty shelves.

When they got home, Dad said that they should have left a note.

Jack looked at the beast, strolling about the orchard, exploring it with paws and noses and sharp eyes.

"I'll go down later," he said – but he knew he wouldn't.

The beast was flinging itself down under the damson trees, and a mosaic of lights was cast upon it by the sun, through a fretwork of leaves. It looked so beautiful like that. It looked so comfortable – so at home – that Jack didn't ever want to let it go. He didn't want to think about the girl and her dad, out there somewhere searching.

It was easier, it was happier, just forgetting.

He managed to forget all day. Indeed, they all did. It was an enchanted day. Mum took the stretch-bandage off Jack's leg, letting the sun on to his white and wrinkled ankle. She pruned her roses, exclaiming that they were surviving after all, thanks to Jack's quick action. Like Emily, she sang.

Emily carried on walking, as if to prove that the first time hadn't been a fluke.

Edward got out his violin and played, not up in the bedroom out of the way, but in the garden for all of them to hear. Jack lay in the hammock, listening to him without any of the usual niggling resentment, which he had never acknowledged before. Edward was a wonderful young musician, and Jack was pleased for him.

Dad finished off the cricket bat and he, Jack and Edward, with unwitting help from Emily, played an inaugural match. At first Jack's ankle felt wonky, and he was terrified of spoiling the day by smashing something. But then he managed to stop worrying. He even began to enjoy himself.

The beast watched them for a while, as if taking in some quaint other-worldly ritual.

Then, to their astonishment, it rose to its feet and joined in. What a beast it was! What a thing! Putting aside its dignity and elegance to flop up and down catching cricket balls in one or another of its mouths like a mere pet. Like one of the family.

In the end even Mum joined in, finishing off the game by bringing out a tray of cold drinks. Dad went into the workshop for his drawing pad. For the rest of the day he sketched the beast: drinking water from the rain-barrel, nicking apples and half-ripe damsons off the trees, looking round at them all with its six pairs of sharp blue eyes, jumping, running, exploring, nuzzling – even sleeping. It was as if he was storing up memories, pages upon pages of them, to keep them going for the rest of their lives.

Mum brought out lunch, including biscuits and tinned meat for the beast, but it sniffed the meat in disgust and walked away to pull down yet more apples from the trees. Everybody laughed. Mum said, "Well, whoever would have thought it?" She looked over Dad's shoulder, and exclaimed that his drawings were better than anything he'd done before; they were inspired. She didn't say anything about the jobs he should be doing in the workshop. About bringing in the money. Nor did she get on with her own jobs, or her gardening.

The beast finished eating apples, and began

to play with Emily. Edward lay on his lazy back, eating a sandwich. Jack held his cricket bat, green from its first play, happy because his ankle had held up, and relieved because he hadn't smashed anything. Perhaps there was hope for him after all, he was thinking. It was a golden day.

Mum came across and stood over him. "I should have believed you about the beast," she said – and it was the nearest she'd ever come to an apology. "I want you to know. Maybe I was tired. I don't know. But the stupidest thing is that I wanted to underneath. Maybe I was envious. Maybe it sometimes seems as if I work so hard and yet all the good things pass me by."

Jack couldn't believe what he was hearing – and neither could Dad.

"It just goes to show," Dad said, leaning towards them both, with a twinkle in his eye. "Some of us aren't perfect all the time!"

Mum pulled a face. Dad laughed. "Nobody's perfect, I know that," she conceded – and, as if to prove the point, she hit him.

They all laughed.

"This is perfect," Jack said, looking at the day going on around them; at the beast, and the garden, and his Mum and Dad who made mistakes and did things wrong – just like him.

Mum lifted her head. She almost seemed to

smell something in the air. "It is," she said, "in its own way. But we must never give up. Can't you feel it, Jack? There's always something out there, always more. Always a treasure yet to work for."

# THE TRANSACTION

They were inside the house at the end of the day. The kitchen door was closed, and the last of the sun shone on to them all, and on to the beast, who lay stretched out on the floor. Jack thought he heard something outside, and he went to see. But the garden was empty.

"Is anything the matter?" Mum said.

There was an edge to her voice, and Jack wondered if she was remembering the grey man again, out there somewhere looking for his beast.

"You didn't just hear anything?" he said.

"No," Mum said.

Jack scoured the empty garden again. Nothing stirred. "I must be getting jumpy," he said.

Mum said that all things considered it wasn't surprising. She was beginning to prepare tea; slowly and meticulously chopping, stirring, simmering, as if holding at bay the dreaded moment when they'd have to take the beast home.

Jack went and helped her. For a while they worked in silence, but then it grew dark and Mum asked him to fetch a candlestick from the front room. It seemed such a shame to turn on the light, she said, with the beast asleep across the floor.

Jack went to the china cabinet and brought out their best candlestick – a silver candelabra which they used for Christmas and special occasions. Passing the window with it, he glanced outside again. He had forgotten the noise on the track, and it came as a shock when he saw a red glow. First it was there, and then it was gone.

He hid behind the curtain, clutching the candelabra to him. When he peered out again, there it still was. Just a tiny point of light among the dark ring of trees which marked their boundary. Anyone else might have missed it. But not him.

"What's taking you so long?" Mum called.

"I'm coming," Jack called back.

He looked again – and the light was gone.

"Perhaps I imagined it," Jack said. But he knew he hadn't.

He took the candlestick into the kitchen. Mum said thank you, but she didn't look up. She was preoccupied with laying the table for their last meal together with the beast – with finding flowers and putting them in a jug, and putting candles in the candelabra, and making everything nice.

Jack left her to it, and crept outside. No point bothering her, he told himself. He closed the door and stood on the drive. At first there was nothing to see, and he didn't know what to do. But then the light glowed again. Still just a tiny point of light, but he saw it.

It's a cigarette, he thought. The way it lights up like that, red and dull. It has to be someone out there, watching us and smoking.

His skin turned prickly cold. Whoever it was between those trees could surely see him. Was it the grey man, he wondered, hunting down his lost beast? And if it was, should he screw up his courage and go and talk to him?

Jack peered among the shadows. His eyes grew accustomed to the dark, and he made out the dark bulk of a car. Its lights were off, but he could see a figure sitting in it. Watching the house, just as he had thought, watching him. Jack shivered.

Suddenly the figure lit another cigarette, and in the little burst of flame, Jack made out the bullish features of – *Uncle Pip*!

Not the grey man or the girl, but Uncle Pip who never gave up on anything!

Of course.

Was Jack relieved, or was he shocked? He didn't have time to find out, for the kitchen door burst open and Mum appeared.

It was like standing in the path of a tornado. As if she had suddenly realized what was going on, Mum started down the drive. She didn't say a thing, but she was very calm, very grim. She reached Jack, but she didn't even look at him. She reminded him of the grey man at the height of his ferocity.

*She's like a mother-tiger,* Jack thought. She knows the hunter's out there, and she knows what he wants. She knows who he is, but it makes no difference. If he tries it on, she'll kill him.

Maybe Uncle Pip thought so too, for suddenly his car exploded into life. Mum bounded towards it, and it backed away from her in a roar of noise and light. Jack hurried after Mum. The car was revving, and struggling and turning to get away. Mum screeched after it. Her eyes were glinting, narrow and bright. The car squealed on to the track, and tomorrow, Jack thought, Uncle Pip would tell himself that it had been the chill of the night that had got to him – that and the loneliness of the Moss, which he had always hated. But he would know, deep down inside, that it was she who had done it. This furious woman. His sister. Jack's mum.

As quickly as he had come, Uncle Pip was gone.

"I hope he ends up in the bog!" Mum said.

At first Jack thought that she was talking to him, but then he turned and saw the beast standing in the kitchen doorway. It looked out with eyes which were sad for once instead of smiling. Jack wondered what it made of them all. He wondered what it was thinking.

"He could have snatched you," Mum said, walking back towards it. "We might tell ourselves it's safe out here, away from everything, but nowhere is."

Dad came to the door. He put his hand on one of the beast's heads, and said, "We must take it home. No wonder they live the way they do. It's not safe to keep it anywhere."

He sounded as if the words were being dragged from him. Plainly he didn't want to let the beast go any more than the rest of them.

Mum reached him. "Let's at least wait until after supper," she said.

They went in, locking and even bolting the door behind them and drawing the curtains tight. The meal was waiting for them on the table, and they began to eat it. Like Emily's singing, it seemed to draw them together as they warded off the moment when the beast would go.

All the while, the beast watched them as if it knew exactly what they were doing. Each of its faces was beautiful in the candlelight, each as much a mystery behind its blue eyes as it seemed they were to it. Dad got to his feet and toasted it in stewed tea. Jack expected that he would never see such blue eyes again.

"We should give it a name to remember it by," said Edward.

Jack shook his head. "Names aren't what's important," he said, remembering what the girl had said. "Some things are beyond names – certainly any names that we could give."

By now the meal was well and truly over. Dad sighed, and said that it was time to go. Edward declared that he'd be up in his room until the thing was done. Mum began to clear the table, head down as if she, too, didn't want to see the beast's departure.

Jack followed Dad outside. "Can I come with you?" he said, unlike Mum and Edward, wanting to stay with the beast for the longest possible time.

"Of course you can," Dad said. He squeezed Jack's shoulder. "I'd appreciate the company."

They began to walk down the lawn, the beast bounding ahead of them, its coat luminous in the dark. Jack remembered the cricket match, all of them out here on a sunny afternoon which had now gone, and the game was over, and the beast was returning home.

They reached the creek, Jack hoping against hope that the girl and her dad would by some miracle have disappeared. But as soon as they reached the inlet he heard the generator throb, and further along the knotweed he heard a kettle whistling and saw a chink of light.

Dad climbed on to the boat and knocked on the cabin roof. Again Jack stood behind him. The kettle came off the boil and there was not a sound inside, not even breathing.

"Don't be afraid," Dad whispered through the crack in the hatch. "We're friends. We mean no harm. We've found your beast."

As if to prove what he was saying, the beast let out the low whine which Jack had first heard under the tarpaulin. Hardly surprisingly, the bolts shot back and the hatch opened. But where Jack had expected the girl or her dad to come bursting out, they stood peering up in the dingy generator light.

For a moment, they all stood like that, as if none of them knew what to do. Then Jack took the initiative. Let's get this over with, he thought, and he went down to them, and the beast followed him.

"Welcome," the girl said, but her voice sounded hollow, it sounded strange; it reminded Jack, somehow, of the way he'd felt that time along the creek, hanging on to his crutch unable to go forward and unable to go back. It sounded *stuck*.

And yet here was her beast, come back again. "May we come in?" Dad said. He wasn't going to let the beast go, just like that. There were things he wanted to know.

The girl stepped aside, and they entered the cabin with the beast. Here, even in the dingy generator light, it seemed to shine.

"What a sight!" Dad said, as if he couldn't help himself. "Isn't it beautiful?"

The man shrugged. "I suppose it is," he said. He shut the hatch behind them, and bolted it.

"You *suppose* it is?" Dad said, widening his eyes.

"There's more to life than beauty," the man said. "I never would have thought it once. But there you are."

Jack looked at the girl, sitting behind him on her unmade bed, and at the dishes in the sink, and at the cold black stove. The place was forlorn, and worse than forlorn. It stank of damp, and pipe tobacco and stale food.

*A little bit of beauty wouldn't go amiss in a place like this,* he thought, catching the girl's eye.

As if she knew what he was thinking, she looked down. "It's been a great adventure," she said. "I wouldn't have changed a minute of it."

For no reason that he could think of, Jack's heart skipped a beat. There was something about the way she said it, sitting there all hunched up. "What is it?" he said.

The girl looked at the beast, now lying between their feet. She said, "The adventure's over. Can't you see? It wants to let us go. It knows the time has come for us to find a proper home."

She said the words "proper home" with such sadness and longing – with such finality – that it went through Jack.

"Tell me where you come from," he said.

The girl sighed. She never once took her eyes off the beast. Jack mightn't have even been there. "It was marvellous at first," she said, remembering. "It came to us one morning. The door was open. Mum was dressed for work and Dad was eating breakfast. Ruby and I were arguing and it just walked in. Where it came from we never knew. It stayed, that's all we cared about. It stayed and changed our lives, and every change was worth it. We wanted it, you see. We'd have done anything to keep it. To look after it. To have it for our own."

"You sound as if you regret it now," Jack said, trying to read the secrets of the girl's voice.

She summoned up a ghost of a smile – and suddenly Jack knew why his heart had skipped a beat. He could feel something. He could feel it coming.

The girl looked at her dad. She said, "Mum told us, long ago, that one day we'd have to let it go. Not that we believed her then, of course. Or that we ever thought we could. But she was right, and so was Ruby. And here we are at long last. Trying to do just that, if you will only help us."

"Help you?" Jack said.

"The time has come for you to take the beast," the girl said. "Can't you feel it?"

In the silence of the moment the kettle began to hiss. Then Dad laughed and said that they couldn't possibly do a thing like that, but Jack laughed too, and said they could; of course they could, if the girl and her dad really meant it.

The girl took the grey man's hand. "Oh, yes," she said. "We mean it."

Jack looked at the man. As if something had ended, he lowered his head.

"Thank you," he said.

Suddenly the transaction was done. Jack looked at the beds and the unwashed dishes, in the flickering, generator light. Now, wherever it was, the girl and her dad could go home.

Excitement shot him through; excitement for them, and excitement for himself, too. The whole world was full of opportunity. It was full of hope.

"Perhaps we'd better go," Dad said, looking as if he didn't know what had hit him.

"It's all quiet outside," the man said, peering between the curtains with a practised eye. "Go quickly; this is your chance."

It was, of course, a taste of things to come.

The overwhelming sense of danger; the furtiveness which would come to haunt them. But Jack didn't know that then. He couldn't have done. The man slid the bolts, and the beast got to its feet as if it understood what was happening. It passed the man by and he said nothing, but the girl touched it wistfully.

"Goodbye," she said, and she sounded lonely; no home as yet, no friends – and now no beast.

"You never told me your name," Jack said, feeling guilty, wanting to offer her something, but not knowing what to give.

"My name's Abalone," the girl said.

Abalone. What sort of a name was that? Jack went out into the night, thinking that they could have been friends in another life.

# THE PRICE

They were gone by morning. Jack went down to the creek with all sorts of silly last-minute questions, and the inlet was empty and all that was left was an envelope tied to the knotweed.

He pulled the envelope to him and opened it. The letter inside said:

*Everything you need to know about the beast:*
1. *It will sleep on anything – it doesn't need a special bed.*
2. *It won't be chained. Don't even think about it.*
3. *It eats apples, in case you haven't found out already.*

Jack laughed. He stuffed the letter into his pocket and returned up the garden. Suddenly it all seemed so simple. The beast was theirs. Day after day from now on, *it was theirs*.

July melted into August, and a golden summer it turned out to be. Edward and Jack broke up from school and the Moss lay waiting for them, vast and empty. They made dens in the old peat channels beneath the shimmering blue sky, played on the flat stones of the dried-up creek, spent lazy hours on the lawn, listening to the skylarks and watching the house martins, always within touch and sight of what they still couldn't believe was their beast.

The only time they came off the Moss was when Dad took them with him to Uncle Pip's, to get rid of the clovers and the rocking-chair.

"That uncle of yours!" Dad exclaimed as they drove away, Uncle Pip still insisting that he knew what he'd seen. "Let's hope your mother's wrath keeps him at bay!"

For a while they worried about whether anything could keep Uncle Pip at bay. In the end, Edward and Jack hung a sign on the garden gate which said:

PRIVATE PROPERTY KEEP OUT
(ESPECIALLY IF YOU'RE UNCLE PIP!!)

and then, as they'd done their best, they forgot him.

It wasn't difficult. The summer rolled on, and there was so much to do. Sure enough, none of their school friends were invited to camp out on the Moss as they usually did in the holidays, but Jack and Edward didn't care.

They didn't even notice, so wrapped up were they in their own lives, and in each other, and in the beast.

Every morning, they awoke and there it was. They'd come downstairs and the sight of it would hit them afresh. Mum would open the back door and out it would go, and she would follow it, and that would be her day. Not fussing as she used to do over housework or her gardening. But watching it. Playing with it. Grooming it. Going where it led. That was her life. That was all their lives.

That is, until autumn came.

Straight away, back at school, Jack noticed the change. Everybody else was sharing their holiday news, and he – who would have joined in once, as a matter of course – didn't have anything to say. Rather, instinctively, he found himself shying away.

"What's up with you?" his friends began to say. And then, "Come to think of it, where've you been hiding yourself all summer?"

Jack told himself that they were exaggerating. Nothing was "up" with him, and he hadn't been hiding. But something was "up" with him. Most definitely.

Every day at school, wherever he was, whatever he was doing, he thought about the beast. Was it all right at home without him? What was it doing now? Could Mum and Dad be trusted to look after it properly?

On and on he worried. He would have loved to bring the beast into school, to keep it close to him. But he could imagine people's shock, pupils and staff alike – imagine their behaviour – and it was more than he dared.

One day, washing his hands in the lavatory, he caught sight of his face. It looked tired and drawn, and it came to him that he'd seen a face like that before. He stared and stared. Sure enough, the eyes weren't quite like the girl's yet – like Abalone's – but they were going that way. His eyes were sad, there was no denying it. It was as if they already knew, though the rest of him refused to, how things would turn out.

He got home that night only to find Edward there with his holdall and violin. He had endured as much as he could stand of music school. He couldn't quite explain why, and Mum and Dad were shocked. They were completely mystified – but Jack understood. Edward said that he didn't even want to play the violin any more, and once Jack wouldn't have cared, but now Edward's words went through him.

He walked into the garden. Dad had made a bonfire, and smoke was rising in a straight line up into a clear sky. The starlings were chattering as they always did at this time of year. The elderberries were dropping. It felt like the end of things.

Jack looked at the few roses which remained after Uncle Pip's battering. Mum hadn't tended them properly in weeks. They were drooping and over-blown, and their dead heads hadn't been nipped. Instead they hung brown and shrivelled on the bush.

Jack looked at the rest of the garden, full of lettuces gone to seed and runner beans which Mum once would have picked for market. This year she had let them grow stringy.

He looked at the workshop, which was empty, no jobs on the go.

Suddenly he realized that the beast was standing in the doorway, looking at these things too. Into Jack's head came the memory of something Abalone had said: *You pay a high price to own a thing like that.*

After tea, the beast and Jack went walking beside the creek. It was an overcast evening, grey and still and getting dark already – but then what else could you expect in September? As they started out, a light rain began to fall like silver mist. A heron flew down the bank ahead of them, settling until they drew near, then flying on again. Jack watched the beast run after it, happy to be wet after the long, dry summer.

By the time they turned back, the night had come on. Thunder rumbled somewhere, and the rain grew heavier. All Jack could see ahead of him was the beast's shining coat. They ran together up the dark lawn, and its eyes weren't blue for once, but as silver as the rain.

When they got indoors, Mum scolded Jack for taking it out. A beast like that was precious, she complained, and it would be his fault if it caught a cold. She was like that, these days. Getting naggy again. Picking on him. She found a pile of towels and began to rub the beast down, complaining that Jack didn't have a clue about looking after things. *He*, who worried about the beast every minute of every day! He tried to tell her about the first time he had seen it, running in the rain. But Mum was too cross and busy to want to know.

Thoroughly disgruntled, Jack decided to go up to bed. Dad was on the phone, turning down the chance to play in some old chums' cricket match. He had been turning things down all summer. Somewhere in the distance, thunder rumbled. Mum took no notice of it, getting on with the drying. The beast looked up at Jack from under the pile of towels. There was something in its eyes. Something sad. It was the last time Jack ever saw it.

Next morning, he came down and the electricity was off owing to the storm, and the beast had disappeared. Mum was beside herself. She'd been at the breakfast table, it seemed, feeding Emily. The door had been open to let in a bit of fresh air, and the beast had strolled outside as it had done a hundred times before – except that when she called, it didn't come. And when she went to see, there was no sign of it.

At first they said that Mum was worrying about nothing and the beast would return. But when it didn't, she began to apportion blame. This was Dad's fault, although she couldn't quite say why. It was certainly Edward's fault for giving up the violin, which the beast had liked to hear him play. It was even her fault for letting it go outside. She should have kept it close by. She had been too casual. She didn't know what she'd been thinking of.

But, most of all, the fault was Jack's. Jack again, who always got things wrong and hadn't taken proper care of it. Jack who had let it out in the rain, and now it had taken itself off to find a better home.

"Maybe someone's stolen it," Jack said, desperate not to be to blame. "Maybe it was Uncle Pip."

But he felt ashamed, even as he said it. For all his faults, Uncle Pip would never do a thing like that.

Mum turned away from him. Her face was pinched. She looked at the house with its threadbare carpets, its walls in need of new paint, its furniture which could have done with replacing if only they could have afforded it. Not the perfect house she had always worked for, but a crummy little one, which had lost its one true treasure, its pearl of great price.

"What are we going to do?" she said.

Later, sitting at his window, watching another bout of storm out on the Moss, Jack remembered something else that Abalone had said.

*The door was open. We were eating breakfast, and it just walked in.*

"It's moved on," he said, suddenly realizing. "It's been through this before. It knows it's more than we can bear, and it's let us go. There's nothing we can do."

His heart went out to it. Poor lonely beast, always moving on because the people that it came to couldn't live with it!

A sheet of lightning lit the Moss. The sky was dark, but it was also golden. Was he sad that the beast was gone – sad for it and sad for him, left behind with an angry mum. Or was he glad?

Just for a moment, he didn't know.

# ABALONE

There was one last thing, one final moment that was so extraordinary that Jack would never forget it. It happened on an ordinary dull day, a January day with nothing beautiful or special to commend it – one of those grey days when Christmas is over and there's nothing to look forward to – when it's too warm for snow and too early for the first snowdrops to hearten with a hope of spring.

They had eaten lunch. Dad lit the fire in the front room, to warm it up for Sunday afternoon tea. Edward went upstairs to practise his violin, which he played again – but with a sadness and depth which he had lacked before.

Left behind, Jack began to romp on the rug with Emily. Always restless, that was him. He gave her rides and she clung on for dear life – making the most of it no doubt, because he was all she'd got now that the beast had gone.

Dad was sleeping on the settee, and Mum came in, wrapped up in herself as she always was these days, carrying the tea things. She passed the window, glancing at the dead heads of the roses which Uncle Pip had damaged in his frenzy and Jack had tried to tie back. The last of them had budded late and it hung there frozen, like a hope unfulfilled.

Mum stopped and looked at it for the longest time. Her face was absolutely still. She might have been made of marble. Suddenly, in a strange, quiet voice, she said, "Jack, come here."

Jack thought she must have seen his bike left out without its cover on. Either that or crisp packets on the drive, or the gate not shut, or his cricket bat abandoned in the long grass. Bracing himself for it, he left Emily playing on the mat and got up to join her at the window.

Nothing in Mum's voice, nothing in her manner, could have prepared him for what he was to see.

The garden was full of beasts. It was quite extraordinary. The afternoon was about to fold in on itself for another day and they were everywhere in the grey light; upon the lawn, in front of the workshop, on the cold black peat, beneath the bare trees.

Where they had come from he would never know, but some of them were standing looking at the house, and some of them were

117

parading up and down, and some of them were hovering – actually hovering – in the huge expanse of winter sky. No two of them were the same. All of them were fabulous. For all their diversity, Jack would never forget a single one.

Nor would he ever be able to describe them. Wings, talons, sinews, every sort of skin from fur, to silver scales, to what looked like silk. But he was seeing them – that was the thing. This was what it meant to have a vision. He knew at last. Not striving for things, hoping until hope had gone, as Mum had done, nor grasping for things in a frenzy of desire as he had done. But, amid the ordinary things of life, unasked for and unheralded, this act of sight.

"Through all the years I sought for something and I didn't know what it was," Mum said. "And now here it is, and all the good things haven't passed me by."

Her eyes filled with tears. Jack wanted to comfort her but he couldn't bring himself to speak. He looked again at the beasts, some animal or bird-like, some almost human, some unlike anything he'd ever seen. Suddenly, to his astonishment, Mum had her arm round him. "I'm sorry, Jack," she said, in a husky voice. "I'm sure you know what I mean."

She turned and looked at him – really looked at him – and Jack knew what she meant, all right. Suddenly he found himself thinking about the door in their kitchen against which he sometimes measured himself. Was he older yet? Was he bigger? Had he really grown? In its own strange way, what was happening now would always be a measure like that. Could he ever expect to be taller, wiser, could he ever expect to be a better person than he was now, before the beasts and in his mother's eyes?

The answer was never better, no, whatever else life might bring. That grey time when he saw the beasts, and Mum saw him, would always be the very best of times.

"As if a veil had been torn from our eyes," Mum murmured, and the beasts stared back at them as if the veil had been torn from their eyes too, and she and Jack were fabulous as well, fabulous and unexpected, standing at their window like pictures framed by life.

That evening, thinking about Abalone for the first time in weeks, wondering if she'd ever seen the creatures too, Jack said, "It's a funny name, Abalone. I wonder where it comes from."

Mum looked up from the window which she'd been staring out of, ever since the beasts had gone, as if the whole world – garden, herons, Moss, creek – as if it *all* was fabulous.

"Abalone?" she said. "It's another kind of pearl, I think you'll find."

"It's a what?" Jack said.

"You collect it off the seabed," Mum said.

Jack thought about her often after that – his other kind of pearl, who might have been a treasure but he had let her friendship go. Where was she now? What was she doing? Did she make a new life? Did she ever think of him as he thought of her, hoping against hope that they'd meet again?

He thought about the beast too, thought about the way it made everything around it luminous. That and its loneliness, always moving on. Did it ever find a home he wondered, or did it go on and on in that story that was never-ending, as Mum had once said? He would never know for sure but he somehow thought it would, as long as there was ever someone out there hoping for a crock of gold, or a pearl of great price.

# A LONG WAY HOME
## by Ann Turnbull

"I won't go to the orphanage, she thought.
I'll never go there. They can't make me."

Since the age of five, Helen has lived at the
Bradleys' with her mother, who served there
as cook. She's never known her father, who
went missing, presumed dead, in the Great
War. Now Mum is dead, taken by the flu,
and Mrs Bradley says Helen must go to live
in an orphanage. But Helen would rather run
away and take her chances on getting a posi-
tion in another house, while she searches for
her father's family...

Set in 1930, this superb novel by the author
of *Pigeon Summer* tells the moving and dra-
matic story of a young girl's valiant search
for a place she can truly call home.

# THE FLOWER KING
by Lesley Howarth

The narrator of this story doesn't just see colours, he *feels* them. At home, the colour is mainly panic-button red. But on Saturdays, visiting old Mrs Pinder, a hopeful yellow floods in. It's the yellow of the daffodil fields where "Pinny" worked as a child for William Bowhays Johns, the Flower King, whose tragic story lies at the heart of this absorbing tale.

Shortlisted for the Whitbread Children's Novel Award and the Guardian Children's Fiction Award.

"Characterization is deft, the descriptive passages lyrical, the dialogue tone perfect."
*Michael Morpurgo, The Guardian*

# MAPHEAD
by Lesley Howarth

Greetings from the Subtle World –

Twelve-year-old MapHead is a visitor from the Subtle World that exists side by side with our own. Basing himself in a tomato house, the young traveller has come to meet his mortal mother for the first time. But, for all his dazzling alien powers, can MapHead master the language of the human heart?

Highly Commended for the Carnegie Medal and the WH Smith Mind Boggling Books Award.

"Weird, moving and funny by turns… Lesley Howarth has a touch of genius." *Chris Powling, Books for Keeps*

"Offbeat and original… Strongly recommended to all who enjoy a good story." *Books For Your Children*

# DON'T MESS WITH ANGELS
## by Susan Gates

"You don't tempt fate. You don't joke about the stone angel."

The stone angel sits on an old gravestone in Thornley churchyard. The grave is said to be that of mad Lord Jago, the subject of a creepy local legend. Alice doesn't believe it, of course, only ... thinking about it gives her the shivers. Her older sister Sarah has no time for such superstition; *her* interest in the grave is strictly scientific. Alice thinks she's crazy. But what at first seems laughable, soon becomes very unfunny indeed. For in the graveyard something is stirring; a terrifying something that threatens to suck the life out of everything – and everyone – it encounters...

## BADGER ON THE BARGE
by Janni Howker

"This set of five stories, each concerned with a relationship between young and old, is quality stuff… Not to be missed." *The Times Educational Supplement*

These fine stories abound with absorbing situations and memorable characters. Meet cussed, rebellious Miss Brady, who lives with a badger on a barge; the reviled old shepherd Reicker; Sally Beck, topiary gardener with an extraordinary past; the reclusive Egg Man; proudly independent Jakey … and the young people whose lives they profoundly affect.

Winner of the International Reading Association Children's Book Award. Shortlisted for the Whitbread` Children's Novel Award and the Carnegie Medal.

## TANGO'S BABY
### by Martin Waddell

Brian Tangello – Tango – is not one of life's romantic heroes. Even his few friends are amazed to learn of his love affair with young Crystal O'Leary, the girl he fancies and who seemed to have no interest in him. Next thing they know, she's pregnant – and that's when the real story of Tango's baby begins. By turns tragic and farcical, it's a story in which many claim a part, but few are able to help Tango as he strives desperately to keep his new family together.

"Stylishly written, sensitive, funny and moving... A book with a depth that can only reward all who read it." *The Times*

"Waddell is as ever an excellent storyteller." *The Independent*

"Brilliantly written." *The Sunday Telegraph*

# MORE WALKER PAPERBACKS
## For You to Enjoy

☐ 0-7445-5496-9   *A Long Way Home* <br> by Ann Turnbull     £3.99

☐ 0-7445-3190-X   *Flower King* <br> by Lesley Howarth     £3.99

☐ 0-7445-5495-0   *MapHead* <br> by Lesley Howarth     £3.99

☐ 0-7445-5490-X   *Don't Mess With Angels* <br> by Susan Gates     £3.99

☐ 0-7445-4352-5   *Badger on the Barge* <br> by Janni Howker     £3.99

☐ 0-7445-5489-6   *Tango's Baby* <br> by Martin Waddell     £3.99

Name _____

Address _____

_____